Go ahead an

No one can hear you. You're no longer in the safe world you know.

You've taken a terrifying step . . .

into the darkest corners of your imagination.

You've opened the door to . . .

Read all the books in

the NIGHTMARE room

series by R.L. Stine

#1 Don't Forget Me!

#2 Locker 13

#3 My Name Is Evil

#4 Liar Liar

#5 Dear Diary, I'm Dead

#6 They Call Me Creature

#7 The Howler

#8 Shadow Girl

the NiGHTMARE room

Shadow Girl

R.L. STINE

※ PARACHUTE PRESS

《Collins

▥ *An imprint of HarperCollinsPublishers*

Shadow Girl

Copyright © 2001 by Parachute Publishing, L.L.C.

Special thanks to Mr. George Sheanshang

First published in the USA by Avon 2001
First published in Great Britain by Collins 2001
Collins is an imprint of HarperCollins*Publishers* Ltd,
77-85 Fulham Palace Road, Hammersmith, London, W6 8JB

The HarperCollins website address is www.fireandwater.com

1 3 5 7 9 8 6 4 2

ISBN 0 00 710456 1

The author asserts the moral right to be identified
as the author of the work

Printed and bound in Great Britain by
Omnia Books Limited, Glasgow

Welcome . . .

Hello, I'm R.L. Stine. I'm here in a little town called Elmwood. Elmwood is a suburb of Chicago—a quiet little town that might look a lot like where you live.

That white, brick house across the street is where our story takes place. Selena Miles is traveling a long way to visit her cousin Jada there. What Selena doesn't know is, that innocent house behind the pretty picket fence holds a secret. Upstairs at the end of the hall stands a room of untold danger and fear.

Selena is climbing the front steps now. Her visit is about to begin. Of course, only you and I know that it's a visit to . . . *THE NIGHTMARE ROOM.*

the NIGHTMARE room

Shadow Girl

Prologue

She rises from the shadows.

She spreads her arms and feels the air lift her off the ground. Her cape billows up, slapping against the wind.

The city spreads beneath her, lights gleaming under a moonless sky. The cold air freezes her cheeks. She ducks her head and swoops low over the empty buildings, the shadowy streets.

Cars seem to be pulled by the twin beams of their headlights. The river flows silently, black as an oil spill.

She is a night bird.

She flies only at night, for her world is a secret world. A secret well kept. No one believes in her or her kind.

She needs to surprise people. And she always does.

She enjoys the startled faces when she drops down from the sky. Her boots land with a hard *thud*, and her cape swirls around her like wings settling around a bird.

The criminals, the punks, the gang members, the thrill seekers—they gasp when they see her. They start to tremble before she says a word or makes a move.

Their faces crumple in defeat. And when they see

the strength of her powers, they sometimes surrender without a fight.

Sometimes.

If they only knew how she felt. Dropping into danger like some kind of crazy deep-sea diver.

Facing their anger, their ugly stares. Facing their weapons. Hoping she will be quick enough to deal with the horrible violence they can unleash.

Behind her mask, they can't see the fear on her face. The billowing cape hides the trembling of her legs. She speaks low so they can't hear her voice shake.

She doesn't know her powers yet. She hasn't learned to trust them. She doesn't know how much strength she can use, or when the mysterious, amazing powers will give out.

But she cannot hide from the challenge. She cannot ignore her mission.

She goes out each night on her lonely patrol.

Looking for trouble . . . and finding it.

Battling the evil. Defeating the lawbreakers.

Yes, it is a special life. Yes, it is thrilling—beyond belief.

But she is also so frightened. So frightened all the time.

You can't blame her—can you?

After all, she's only twelve.

"Every time I picture Jada I want to barf," I told Beth. "That perfect round face. That perfect blond hair. The big blue eyes. Those little red lips that always seem to be sneering at me. Yuck."

Beth laughed. "Selena, when is the last time you saw your cousin?"

I had to think. "I guess it was six years ago."

Beth's dark eyes flashed. "So you were both six—right?"

I nodded.

"And now you're twelve," Beth continued.

I snickered. "You always were a math genius. How did you do that without a calculator?"

"Ha-ha." Beth rolled her eyes. She is my best friend, but she never laughs at my jokes.

We were up in my room, discussing my cousin Jada. The suitcase was open on my bed. I was supposed to be packing. But I didn't feel like it. I *really* didn't want to go stay with Jada for a month.

Beth pulled the red scrunchie from her wavy brown hair and let her hair fall over her shoulders. She sat on the floor with her knees pulled up, and rested her elbows on her knees.

"Your cousin has probably changed in six years," she said.

"She probably got meaner," I muttered. "I'll bet she grew claws, and her parents had to get her a scratching post."

Beth didn't laugh.

I could hear Mom slamming cabinet doors in the kitchen. Mom never closes doors. She always slams them. I tell her she doesn't know her own strength. But I think it's because she's always in such a hurry.

She is a phone company supervisor. She works all night. So she doesn't have much time to waste during the day.

I knew she'd come upstairs soon and get on my case about packing for my trip.

Beth sighed. She sprawled back on the white shag rug. "I don't understand, Selena. Jada was only six when you saw her last. So how mean could she be?"

"Pretty mean," I said. "She cut off one of my pigtails when I was sleeping. Then she told Mom that she saw *me* do it. Is that mean enough?"

Beth nodded. "Pretty mean. Did your mom figure out the truth?"

I shook my head. "Mom was too upset. Too busy trying to think of how to fix my hair."

"What happened?"

"Mom got me a really short haircut. Like a boy's. I cried for weeks about it. Jada thought it was so funny. She laughed at me and tapped my head with her fist whenever Mom wasn't looking."

"That's awful," Beth agreed.

"Oh. I just remembered something else," I said. "Jada called me Moo Cow."

Beth's mouth dropped open. "Excuse me?"

"She called me Moo Cow all the time. It made me so angry. 'Moo Cow, let's do this' and 'Moo Cow, let's do that.'"

Beth frowned at me. "I don't get it. Why Moo Cow?"

I shrugged. "I'm not sure. I guess it was because she was so skinny and I was so much bigger, I looked like a cow to her."

"Nice," Beth muttered. "Well, you're thin now, Selena. She won't be able to call you that anymore. And maybe she blimped up in six years."

"No way," I said sadly. "I saw her Christmas photo. She looks like a broom with blond hair."

"Well, she's probably a lot nicer," Beth said, climbing to her feet. "She emailed you, right?"

I nodded. "Yeah. She said she couldn't wait for me to get there. But she spelled my name with two Ls. That couldn't be a mistake, Beth. That had to be deliberate."

"Well . . . I'm going to miss you," Beth said. "Who

3

else is going to make me laugh?"

Laugh? I'd never seen Beth laugh once! What was she talking about?

It didn't matter. Before I knew it, we were hugging each other, and I had tears burning my eyes. "I'll email you five times a day," I said.

Beth dropped onto the edge of my bed. "I still don't understand why you have to go for a whole month," she said. "It's April. School will almost be over when you get back."

"I have to go to Jada's school," I sighed.

"But *why*?" Beth asked.

I shrugged. "Mom is being totally weird about it. She says my cousin needs me."

Beth sat up straight. "Huh? Is Jada sick or something?"

"Beats me," I said. "Mom won't say. She just says we need a vacation from each other anyway."

"Totally weird," Beth muttered.

Mom's shout from downstairs broke into our conversation. "Hey, girls—how is the packing going up there?"

I stared at the empty suitcase. "Fine," I called down. "Almost finished."

The bus was already boarding the next morning when Mom and I arrived. We ran through the crowded station. Mom carried one of my bags. I carried the other. My bulging backpack bounced on my shoulders.

It had rained all morning, and the concrete floor was slippery and wet. Two little girls were crying beside the ticket booth. A young man with long, greasy hair sat playing a guitar on the floor.

Mom and I stopped by the gate. She dropped the suitcase beside me and handed me my ticket.

I bit my bottom lip to keep my chin from trembling. I hadn't expected to be this nervous. I guess it was because Mom and I are so close. We used to fight a lot. But ever since Dad died, we haven't had a cross word between us.

I turned to Mom. "I'll call you as soon as I get to Aunt Janet's," I said.

She nodded. "Yes. Tell my sister I'm sorry I can't be there." She took a deep breath. "I . . . I wrote you a letter."

"A letter?"

She nodded, then wrapped me in a hug. Such a tight hug. She hugged me so hard, I could barely breathe.

I started to pull away. But she wouldn't let go.

She pressed her hot cheek against mine. To my surprise, my face became wet.

When Mom finally let go, I saw tears streaming down her face.

I gasped in surprise. My mom never cries. Never. Even when Dad died, I didn't see her cry.

I wanted her to stop. It was upsetting me—a lot. "Hey, it's only a month," I said.

A loud sob escaped her open mouth. And then more tears flowed from behind her glasses.

"Mom—what's wrong?" I asked. "Why are you crying? Mom—answer me. Why are you crying like that?"

I thought about Mom as the bus bounced along the highway to Chicago.

She didn't answer my question at the bus station. She didn't explain why she suddenly became so emotional. Instead, she turned and ran away.

Weird.

I watched her run through the crowd. She caught her purse on the arm of a bench and had to struggle to pull it free. Then she ran out of the station.

She didn't look back.

Not once.

I rubbed my face. It was still damp from her tears. I could smell her makeup on my skin.

Swallowing hard, I picked up my bags and made my way to the bus.

I found a seat at the back and stared out the steamy window at the gray, rain-soaked day. No one sat next to me. So I was able to stretch out a bit.

Jada lived with her parents—my aunt Janet and

Uncle Will—in a suburb called Elmwood a few miles outside Chicago. I had been to her house only once, when I was two or three. But I had seen pictures of it plenty of times.

It was small—a square white brick box with a tiny strip of front lawn. White picket fences separated Jada's house from the little houses on both sides.

I didn't know my aunt and uncle very well. Aunt Janet was a school librarian. Uncle Will worked for the Chicago Cubs. I'm not sure what he did for them.

They always called on my birthday and at Christmas. But I hadn't seen either of them since I was six.

Sitting in the back of the bus, listening to the rain drum on the metal roof, I suddenly felt very alone. I pulled my jacket tighter and slumped down in the seat.

Outside, the whole world was gray. Cars all had their headlights on. But the pale beams of light barely seemed to cut through the gloom.

The man in the seat in front of me began snoring loudly. Across from him, two kids bundled up in snowsuits despite the heat of the bus began to giggle.

"It's going to be okay, Selena," I told myself, pressing my forehead against the cool window glass. "You and Jada are going to be best pals. Like sisters."

I was so wrong.

It was late afternoon when the taxi pulled up in front of Jada's house. The rain had stopped, but dark gray clouds still floated low across the sky. The narrow street was wet and puddled.

I paid the driver and started to climb out of the car.

"Hey—you're here!" Aunt Janet came running down the front stoop, clapping her hands.

I hadn't remembered how tiny and thin she was. Dressed in black slacks and a black T-shirt, she looked like an excited blackbird.

Her short black hair, streaked with blond, bobbed on her head as she came running down the walk. "Hey—Selena—it's you!"

"In person!" I declared, grinning back at her.

I had started to pick up my suitcases. But I had to drop them to the pavement as Aunt Janet threw her scrawny arms around me in a hug.

"Jada is so excited!" she told me. "She can't *wait* to see you."

"I can't wait to see her," I said. "I can't believe I'm really here! It's been so long."

"Will is still at work," she said, grabbing up one of my bags. "But he'll be home for dinner. He has a lot of fun things planned for us all in the city."

She had tiny round blackbird eyes. They studied me for a brief moment. "It's so nice to have you here," she said. When she smiled, her eyes crinkled into a hundred little lines at the corners.

She hugged me again. "Go on. Go upstairs to Jada's room. She's waiting for you." She waved me toward the front door. "I'll bring in your bags. Go ahead. Shoo."

I hesitated. I thought the suitcases might be too heavy for my aunt. But she waved me away again. So I went running into the house.

I glanced into the small living room. A TV was on in the corner. Oprah was holding up a book and talking to a group of serious-looking women.

I took a deep breath. The house smelled of chocolate. Through the doorway to the kitchen, I could see a tall chocolate cake on the counter.

What a nice welcome, I thought. Aunt Janet seemed really glad to see me.

I took another deep breath and ran up the stairs to Jada's room. My heart started to pound as I reached the landing.

Jada's room wasn't hard to find. There were only a few rooms upstairs. The doors were all closed except for the one at the end of the hall.

"Jada—I'm here!" I called.

I stepped into the room. I saw two twin beds on one wall, separated by a small dresser.

A boy with short brown hair sat on the edge of one of the beds. He was dressed in baggy cargo pants and an oversize black T-shirt that had the words "Rock & Roll Forever" on the front. He grinned up at me from the magazine he had in his lap.

Jada stood on the other side of the room, facing the window. She was so tall and thin!

We were the same age—only a month apart. But Jada was at least five or six inches taller than me.

Her light blond hair was pulled back and tied with a blue, ribbony scrunchie. She wore a blue-and-red-striped top pulled down over straight-legged jeans that made her legs look a mile long.

"Jada—hi! I made it!" I cried. I started across the room to her.

She spun around. "Can't you see I'm on the phone?"

"Oh. Uh—" I stopped short—and saw the tiny, silvery cell phone pressed to her ear. "Sorry."

She turned back to the window and continued to talk into the phone.

The boy tossed his magazine onto the bed. "How's it going?" he asked. "You're Jada's cousin, right? She said you were coming today. I'm Stan."

"Hi, Stan." I stood awkwardly in the middle of the

room. I suddenly didn't know what to do with my hands. I was wearing a leather skirt, so I didn't have any pockets to shove them in.

Jada still had her back to me. She picked up a tennis ball from a shelf and squeezed it in one hand as she talked into the phone.

"You came up on the bus?" Stan asked. "How was it?"

"Not bad," I said. "We were stuck in a lot of traffic when we passed the airport."

I felt like a geek. Why was I talking about *traffic*?

"So you're going to stay here for a whole month?" Stan asked. "Guess you and Jada will be sharing this room."

"I guess," I replied, glancing around the small, cluttered room. "Hope Jada doesn't mind."

"Hope Jada doesn't mind *what*?" my cousin demanded.

I turned to see that she had finally put down the phone. Her blue eyes studied me. She had purple lipstick on her lips. She was absolutely beautiful. Like a supermodel.

"Hope you don't mind sharing your room," I answered her question.

She shrugged. "Whatever." Then the purple lips spread into a smile, and she stepped forward to hug me.

"It's great to see you," I said.

"Moo Cow—I can't believe you're here!" she exclaimed.

My mouth dropped open. "Excuse me? What did you—"

"Moo Cow! Moo Cow!" she repeated gleefully.

Stan laughed. "Why are you calling her that?" he asked Jada. "Is that a nickname or something?"

"Moo Cow?" Jada repeated. "It's what I've always called her."

I could feel my face grow hot and knew I was blushing. I balled my hands into tight fists. "But—why?" I asked.

Jada shook her head. Her blue eyes flashed. "Don't you remember? When we were little kids, and I was visiting you?"

"Remember what?"

"You fell down the stairs," Jada replied. "You said I pushed you, but that wasn't true. You fell and you started to cry. But it wasn't like normal crying. It sounded just like a cow mooing."

"I—I don't remember that," I stammered.

"Of course you do," Jada said, grinning. "I called you Moo Cow ever since."

Stan laughed. "Go ahead. Do it," he said to me. He jumped to his feet. "Can you still do it? Moo like a cow?"

"No way!" I cried. I knew I was blushing even harder. "I don't know what she's talking about. Really!"

"Oh, go ahead," Jada said. She tossed back her head and began to moo. A really sick moo that sounded more like someone choking, gasping for air.

Stan joined in, and the two of them mooed at the top of their lungs at each other.

"Is this what you do for fun up here?" I said. "Maybe we could work on some other barnyard animals and enter a talent show."

They finally stopped mooing. Jada's eyes flashed excitedly. She grinned at me. "We're going to have a great time!"

"Not if you keep calling me Moo Cow," I warned.

Jada started to reply. But a loud clumping noise on the stairs made her stop.

We heard a scream. "Help me! Jada—help me!" a girl moaned.

Jada's eyes went wide.

I spun around to face the door.

A tall girl with curly red hair staggered into the room. She was gasping for breath, her eyes rolling crazily in her head.

I cried out when I saw the red trickle of blood down the side of her face.

"Help me!" she wailed. "Ohhh. . . . please help!"

"Cindy—what *happened*?" Jada cried.

She rushed across the room and helped her to the edge of the bed.

"I—I was robbed!" the girl sobbed. She raised a hand to the bleeding cut on the side of her head.

I suddenly felt queasy. The sight of blood always makes me sick. I can't stand violence of any kind. I always have to shut my eyes at the scary parts of movies.

"Cindy? I thought that was you! What on earth—!" Aunt Janet rushed into the room. She dropped down beside Cindy and examined her cut. "It's not too bad," she said. "I think we can stop the bleeding pretty easily."

She ran out of the room and returned a few seconds later with a wet washcloth. She gently pressed it against Cindy's temple.

"I—I went to the cash machine for my mom," Cindy said, still breathing hard. "But as soon as I got the cash, these men appeared. Three of them. They stepped in front of me. They didn't say a word."

"Wow. That's so scary," Stan muttered. He stood beside the bed with his hands shoved deep in his pockets. He had suddenly grown very pale.

My stomach lurched. I swallowed hard, trying to keep from throwing up.

Jada sat on the other side of Cindy, patting her shoulder. Aunt Janet continued to mop her temple gently. Dried blood had caked in Cindy's red hair.

"I had no choice. I gave them my wallet," Cindy said, her voice trembling. "But they threw me down on the sidewalk. Then they took off. I—I started to run home. But I was so upset, I ran into a tree. That's how I cut myself."

"The bleeding is slowing," Aunt Janet said softly. "I don't think you'll need stitches." She put the cloth in Cindy's hand. "Hold it against your head. I'm going to go phone your mother."

"What about the police?" Jada asked.

"Cindy's mom can call the police after they get home," Aunt Janet said. She hurried from the room.

Jada had her arm around her friend. "You're going to be okay," she said softly. "Did you get a good look at the men?"

"No. They had hats pulled down low on their heads. They were real tough-looking. I—I was so scared," Cindy whispered. "Luckily, I realized I was only a few blocks from your house."

Jada suddenly turned to me. "Wouldn't you *love* to be some kind of superhero?" she asked. "You could swoop out the window and go round up those three creeps."

The idea made my stomach lurch again. "No way," I replied. "I'd be too terrified."

Jada stared at me, frowning. I had the feeling I'd said something wrong.

I turned to Cindy. "By the way, I'm Jada's cousin Selena," I said.

"Hi," Cindy said, mopping at her wound. The washcloth was stained with red now. "Jada said you were coming."

"Yeah," I said awkwardly. I had been standing tensely in the corner with my arms crossed tightly in front of me. "I—I'm sorry about . . . what happened."

Cindy didn't hear me. She and Jada were already talking to each other in soft whispers.

"It's kind of creepy. There has been a whole bunch of robberies in this neighborhood," Stan told me.

"Whoa. That's awful," I replied.

"Welcome to Chicago," Jada said bitterly.

A few minutes later, Jada and Stan led Cindy downstairs. I dropped onto the edge of the bed and shut my eyes. I felt dizzy and sick. I kept picturing the three men robbing Cindy.

After a short while, I began to feel better. I picked up Cindy's washcloth and started to carry it to the bathroom. I stopped halfway down the hall.

"Whoa." The red stains on the cloth were so bright. Not dark like blood.

I raised the cloth to examine it. Paint. It smelled like paint.

Yes. The stains were red paint—not blood.

I stared at the cloth, feeling dizzy again. Was Cindy faking the whole thing? I wondered.

No. No way. Why would she do that?

The four of us sat around the table in the small dining room. Aunt Janet passed the platter of fried chicken to me.

"I'll bet you girls would like to go shopping on Saturday," Uncle Will said. "I could drive you into the city and drop you off on Michigan Avenue."

"All of the great stores are there," Aunt Janet told me.

"Sounds awesome," I said. I looked across the dinner table at Jada.

"I might have some other stuff to do Saturday," Jada said, staring back at me coldly. "With my friends."

Uncle Will swallowed a forkful of mashed potatoes. "You haven't seen Selena since you were little. I know you two will want to get to know each other."

"This chicken is totally delicious," I told Aunt Janet. I really wanted to change the subject.

Up until Jada's comment, dinner had been really nice. It was great to see Uncle Will again.

He was a chubby, round man with bright red cheeks, a twinkle in his blue-gray eyes, a thick nest of black hair bobbing on his head, and a big, booming voice.

I didn't remember too much about him from when I was a kid. But he was so warm and friendly, I knew we were going to get along great.

"Hey—" I dropped my fork and knife to the table. "I forgot to phone Mom," I said. "I should call and tell her I arrived."

I saw Jada gasp. She turned to her mother as if I had said something wrong.

"No need, Selena," Aunt Janet said. "I already called your mom. This afternoon. I told her you were here safe and sound."

"Well, I'd just like to call her and tell her how great everything is," I said. I pushed back my chair and started to stand up. "I want to tell her about the great dinner she's missing."

"Uh . . . wouldn't she be at work by now?" Aunt Janet asked.

I glanced at my watch. "No. Not for another hour," I said.

"Sit down," Uncle Will urged softly, waving me down with both hands. "Enjoy your dinner, Selena. Don't worry. You'll talk to your mom later."

I lowered myself slowly onto my chair.

Jada rolled her eyes. "You *can't* be homesick already!"

"Hey, have you ever had real Chicago deep-dish pizza?" Uncle Will asked, grinning at me. "I'll bet you haven't. Well, I know the greatest place. It's near Northwestern University. Maybe I'll take everyone there tomorrow night."

"Excellent," I said. I gazed down at my plate. Suddenly, I wasn't hungry anymore.

Am I just imagining it? I asked myself. Or were they really trying to keep me from calling Mom?

"Mine's the bed by the window," Jada said. "I like a lot of fresh air."

"Okay," I replied. I glanced out the window into the night. Strong wind gusts sent curtains of rain spattering against the glass.

I felt totally stuffed. Uncle Will had insisted that I have two slices of Aunt Janet's chocolate cake!

Now I had a suitcase open on my twin bed and had started to unpack.

Jada stood across the bed from me, hands at her waist, shaking her head. "I can't believe you brought *two* suitcases," she said.

She is really being unpleasant, I thought. Trying to make me feel bad. "Well, I *am* staying a whole month," I said. "And I didn't know how cold it is here in April."

Jada sighed. "I cleared out a dresser drawer for you." She pulled open the bottom dresser drawer. Then she walked over to the closet and tugged open the door. "The closet is pretty full. But I guess you

22

can squeeze some stuff in."

I stared into the closet. It was jammed from wall to wall with Jada's clothes. Not a spare inch.

And *one* measly dresser drawer?

"Uh . . . I guess I'll keep some of my stuff in a suitcase," I muttered.

Jada didn't reply. She sat down at her desk and punched a number into the phone. "Hey, Stan. What's up?"

She and Stan discussed Cindy for a while. Then they started talking about some teachers at school.

While she talked, I pulled out clothes I thought I'd need right away and jammed them into the dresser drawer.

"Jada?" Aunt Janet called from downstairs. "Are you helping Selena unpack?"

Jada lowered the phone from her ear. "Yes, I am!" she shouted back. "We're doing great!" Then she went back to talking to Stan.

I pulled a straight, plaid skirt out from the suitcase. I held it up and tried to smooth some of the wrinkles out.

Jada clicked off the phone. She turned around in her desk chair and started to laugh.

"What's so funny?" I asked.

"Wow. I had that same skirt in third grade!" she sneered.

I held it up in front of me. "Do you think it's too young?"

"For you?" Jada replied. "No."

I wanted to wipe the sick grin off her face.

Why was she being so horrible to me?

I'm going to be here a whole month, I thought, suddenly feeling very worried. I'm going to be sharing this tiny bedroom with her.

I really want to get along. I really want her to like me.

"I . . . I hope you and I can finally get to know one another," I stammered.

Jada ignored me. She didn't answer. She squatted in front of her bookcase and started to search for something. A minute later, she crossed the room to me, carrying a stack of comic books.

"Are you into these?" she asked.

My mouth dropped open. I couldn't hide my shock. "*You* read comic books?"

She nodded. "Yeah. I love them."

I lowered my eyes to them. "What kind do you read? Graphic novels?"

"No way." She pushed the stack of comics into my chest. "Here. Check them out."

I took the pile from her and flipped through them. They were all comics about female superheroes. *Silver Katt, Marla Mutant, Fox Woman,* and one called *Super Model,* about a beautiful young woman who uses her fabulous good looks to hypnotize bad guys.

They looked kind of babyish to me. But I muttered, "Interesting."

Jada snickered. "I don't tell too many people I read comics. Girls aren't supposed to read them, right?"

"It's a little weird," I replied.

She sighed. "But wouldn't it be cool if super-heroes really existed?"

I stared at her. Why does she keep talking about superheroes? I wondered.

I finished unpacking. I had to leave most of my clothes in the suitcases. Then I shoved the suitcases under the bed.

I suddenly felt exhausted. I guess from the long bus ride.

I said good night to my aunt and uncle. Jada said she was tired too. A few minutes later, the two of us were lying silently in our twin beds. I stared up at the darkness, listening to the unfamiliar noises of the house.

Before long, I fell into a deep, dreamless sleep.

I awoke sometime later. I glanced at the clock radio on the bed table. Three-fifteen in the morning.

I turned onto my other side—and blinked in surprise when I glimpsed Jada's bed.

Empty.

Her bed was empty.

The next morning—my first day at Jada's school—I couldn't decide what to wear. Should I wear jeans and my new blue sweater? Or my leather skirt with a vest or something?

I was still staring at the skirt and my sweater when Jada came out of the bathroom, drying her hair with a big bath towel. "It's all yours," she said. "Sorry I steamed it up a little."

"Where did you go last night?" I blurted out.

She narrowed her blue eyes at me. "Excuse me?"

"I woke up and you were gone," I said.

She scowled. "Are you *spying* on me? I went downstairs for a glass of water. Is that a big deal?"

She was gone a lot longer than that, I told myself.

Jada pulled off the towel and shook out her hair. "Oh, wow. I almost forgot. Today is Spirit Day."

"It's *what*?" I asked.

"Spirit Day. It's like a big pep rally in the gym first thing this morning. You know. For our basketball

26

team—the Golden Bears."

"But isn't basketball season over?" I asked.

Jada nodded. "But we always have Spirit Day to honor the team. We went to the state tournament this year." She moved past me to the closet. "You have to wear green and gold. Everyone wears green and gold today."

I blinked. "Green and gold? Well . . ." I thought hard about the clothes I brought. "I have a pair of green corduroy slacks."

"Great," Jada said, reaching onto the closet shelf to pull down a yellow sweater. "I'm wearing this sweater with a green corduroy skirt. You know what? I have a green vest you could wear."

I gazed at her long, skinny body. "Think it would fit me?"

"Of course," she replied. "If you keep it open. Do you have a yellow top you can wear under it?"

"I think so," I said.

A few minutes later, I waved good-bye to Aunt Janet and followed Jada out the door.

It was a blustery, gray day. The trees swayed and creaked in the wind. I zipped my down coat up to my chin and shoved my hands into the pockets.

Jada's school—Elmwood Middle School—was two blocks away. Jada walked quickly, taking long strides. I had to jog to keep up with her.

She had a strange smile on her face. And once, I caught her giggling about something. "What's so funny?" I asked.

She shrugged. "Just thinking about something."

We were a little late. Most kids had already gone into the school.

It was a low redbrick building that stretched for nearly a block. I could see a football field with bleachers on the right. In front, the flag whipped and slapped against itself in the blowing wind.

I was happy to step inside the building. Even though we'd walked only two blocks, my face was burning from the cold.

I suddenly thought about Mom. I wanted to call her before breakfast. But she had been working all night. I decided not to wake her up.

The yellow-tiled halls were nearly empty. I could hear voices ringing out in the gym down the hall. A boy ran past and yelled to Jada, "You're late. Better hurry."

"Let me take your coat, since you don't have a locker," Jada said, reaching for it. "The gym is right down there." She pointed in the direction of the voices. "I'll put your coat in my locker and meet you there."

I handed her my coat, and she took off. "Save me a seat!" she called.

I straightened the green vest. And pulled down the sleeves of my yellow shirt. Then I pushed open

28

the gym doors and walked inside.

I stepped into a roar of voices. Shouts and laughter swept down from the tall bleachers and echoed off the gym walls.

Cheerleaders huddled together on the floor in front of the bleachers. I gazed up to the top. Just about every seat was taken.

I spotted a space at the very top and started to climb the metal stairs. I had climbed only a few steps, when the gym suddenly grew silent.

I thought it was because the pep rally was about to begin. I didn't realize it was quiet because of me.

Not until I heard the first shouts.

"Blakemoor girl!"

"Booooo!"

"Get out of here, Blakemoor! You don't belong here!"

"Booooo! Who invited her?"

"Get out! Get outta here!"

It took me so long to realize they were shouting at *me*.

My heart stopped. I turned and I saw—

I saw . . .

I saw how they were all dressed. All down the bleacher rows. The whole gym. Everyone . . .

Everyone dressed in red and blue.

Red and blue. I knew in a second. I knew what Jada had done to me.

Red and blue were the school colors at Elmwood.

And I was wearing yellow and green.

"Out! Out! Out!" The whole gym was chanting now. The bleachers rocked. Kids jumped to their feet. Clapping as they chanted.

"Out! Out! Out!"

I turned back to the gym floor and nearly fell. My foot caught on the metal step. I swung my arms and caught my balance.

"Out! Out! Out!"

I knew I was blushing like crazy. I jumped down the few steps to the floor.

And saw Jada enter at the other side of the gym. She was wearing red and blue. She must have changed after she took my coat.

She flashed me a big grin and started to climb into the bleachers.

"Out! Out! Out!"

"Get Blakemoor out!"

A teacher had stepped up to the microphone on the gym floor. He waved his hands in the air and shouted for everyone to calm down.

In their red-and-blue uniforms, the cheerleaders stood in a line, staring at me.

"Out! Out! Out!" Stamping and clapping. The chant grew louder.

I let out a loud cry. I didn't know what to do. Where to turn.

Holding my hands over my ears, I spun away from the bleachers and ran.

Out the gym door. Down the long, empty hall. Back outside.

No coat. Jada had hidden my coat somewhere so that the whole school would see. Everyone would see the wrong school colors I was wearing.

The whole school would always remember that I was the girl who wore green and yellow on her first day at Elmwood. Everyone would see me and remember. How was I going to survive a whole month here?

With a cry, I started to run. The wind blew dead leaves against me, as if trying to push me back. I lowered my head into the wind and ran.

Down the school walk.

Into the street.

A car horn blared. I didn't look up. My shoes pounded the street. The wind blew my hair up behind me.

Where was I running? I didn't know. I just had to get away.

I didn't know there was no escape.

No escape from Jada and the terrifying plans she had for me.

I ran the two blocks back to Jada's house. By the time the little white house came into view, I was shivering from the cold.

I'll change my clothes, I decided.

Then I'll go back to the school and pretend that nothing happened.

I climbed the front stoop and pounded on the door.

How will I ever pay Jada back for that mean trick? I asked myself. "I'll think of something," I said out loud.

"Open up!" I pounded on the door again. I pressed the doorbell, holding the button down. I could hear it buzzing inside.

"Come on, Aunt Janet. Come on!"

I hugged myself to stop my shivers. The wind whipped around the side of the house, nearly pushing me off the stoop.

Silence inside. I buzzed again. I tried the door. Locked tight.

No one home. My aunt must have gone out.

I realized I didn't have a key.

Another blast of wind sent me hopping off the stoop. I have no choice, I decided. I can't stand out here all day without my coat. I have to go back to school. Even in this awful, embarrassing green and yellow outfit.

So I ran to the street and raced back to school. By the time I stepped into the warmth of the building, my whole face was numb and my skin was absolutely blue!

I had no idea where to go. I had to wander the halls until I found the principal's office. The secretary looked me up in the computer. Then she took me by the hand and led me to my classroom.

Of course everyone stared as I stepped hesitantly into the room. I glanced quickly across the room. Everyone in red and blue.

I spotted Jada in the front row. She flashed me another big grin.

That grin made me want to explode. Violence makes me sick. But I wanted to run over there and punch her face until it was red and blue too!

Instead, I introduced myself to Miss Colgate, my new teacher.

She smiled and said, "Hi, Selena. Welcome." But her eyes were on my outfit. "I'm afraid you picked the wrong colors to wear today."

The teacher turned to Jada. "Jada, you should

have warned your cousin about what to wear," she scolded.

"I tried to," Jada replied, still grinning. "But she wouldn't listen."

"That's not true!" I cried. It came out much more shrill than I intended. I sounded like a whining baby.

Miss Colgate pointed me to an empty desk. I could feel all eyes on me as I slunk across the room and dropped into the chair.

I wanted to vanish into the floor. I wanted to be invisible.

Why doesn't Jada want to be my friend? I wondered.

Why does she want to be my enemy?

After school, I couldn't wait to get home. I started to walk to the front door of the school, but Stan moved to block my way.

He wore a brown leather bomber jacket. The leather was streaked and stained, and one pocket was nearly torn off. He tugged a wool ski cap down over his ears.

"Guess you had a bad day," he said.

I nodded. "It wasn't the greatest."

"Sometimes Jada's jokes can be kind of mean," he said.

"Kind of," I muttered. I pushed open the door and stepped outside.

"I think she's stressed about you staying with

her," Stan said. "I mean, she doesn't know you or anything."

"Well, she isn't exactly trying to *impress* me!" I cried.

I waved and trotted away. Wrapping my coat around me, I hurried home. I couldn't wait to change out of the awful clothes.

Aunt Janet let me in. "How was your first day at Elmwood?"

"Don't ask," I groaned. I hurried up to the bedroom I shared with Jada.

I dropped to the floor and pulled my suitcase out from under my bed. I opened the lid. Leaning over it, I pulled out a pair of faded denim jeans and a gray sweatshirt.

I started to close the suitcase. Then I saw a white envelope tucked between some sweaters. A letter. Yes. The letter my mom said she wrote to me. I had forgotten all about it.

I dropped the jeans and sweatshirt. Pulled out the envelope. Ripped it open and unfolded the letter.

As I began to read, my hand started to tremble. My heart started to pound. I had to hold the letter in both hands to keep it steady.

No. No . . . ! *This can't be real,* I thought. My mom didn't write this—*did* she?

Dear Selena,

Soon you will learn the truth.

You will know why I acted so strangely, why I was so sorry to say good-bye to you.

Your mind will be spinning with all you have found out.

The hardest part is knowing that things will never be the same.

It will be hard for you. And it is terribly hard for me.

You are on your own now. You must make your own way.

Please, please forgive me, Selena.

Don't think of your life with me as a lie. Try to understand why I couldn't tell you the truth.

Try to understand why I could never reveal what I knew. Even though it was on my mind, day and night.

I know it's hard. But you must know that this is even more painful for me than it is for you.

I will miss you and love you always.

Don't forget me.

Your Mom

I was on my knees on the floor, reading the letter for the third time, when Jada burst into the room.

She tossed her coat and backpack onto her bed, then turned to me. "What's up? What are you doing down there?"

I held the letter up. My hand was still shaking.

The words in the letter didn't make any sense to me. No sense at all.

What was my mother talking about?

"This letter—" I started to tell Jada about it. But then I stopped. And stared up at her as a wave of anger swept over me.

"How could you *do* that to me?" I shrieked. "How could you play such a rotten trick on my first day of school?"

She had started to twist her blond hair into a ponytail. But she stopped and let her hair fall over her shoulders. A grin spread slowly over her face. "It was pretty funny," she murmured.

"Huh? *Funny?*" I shrieked, jumping to my feet. "Jada—how can you be so *cold!*"

And then I exploded.

I leaped at her. And wrapped my arms around her scrawny waist. Tackled her. And sent her sprawling on her back onto her bed.

With a startled cry, she pulled herself up quickly. She raised both hands to protect herself.

But I jumped at her again. And before I realized what I was doing, I was wrestling with her.

Jada stumbled over my open suitcase. I gave her a hard shove and pushed her to the floor. Then I threw myself on top of her, screaming at the top of my lungs, "Why are you so horrible? *Why?*"

"Stop! Stop this—right now!"

Aunt Janet's shrieks from the doorway made us both freeze.

"What on earth—!" my aunt exclaimed, both hands pressed to the sides of her face.

I stood up, panting like a dog, my heart hammering in my chest. My hair was damp from sweat. I blew a strand from over my eye.

Jada stayed on the floor. Straightening her T-shirt, she sat up slowly. "We . . . we were just kidding around," she choked out.

Aunt Janet uttered a cry. "Kidding around?"

"Yeah. Really, Mom," Jada said.

"We weren't really fighting." I took up Jada's lie. "Just wrestling around. You see, I was a little angry.

And I guess . . . well . . ."

Aunt Janet lowered her hands to her waist. She gazed at us both suspiciously. "Why were you angry, Selena?" she asked.

I glanced at Jada. "Well . . . Jada played kind of a mean trick on me this morning. It was Spirit Day at school, see. And Jada told me to wear this." I motioned to the green vest, which was twisted around me from our wrestling match. My yellow T-shirt, green slacks.

Aunt Janet stared at my outfit. Then she burst out laughing. "Jada told you to wear green and gold?"

I nodded.

My aunt shook her head. "Jada and her sick sense of humor," she said, chuckling. "I don't know where she gets it from. It must be from Will's side of the family. My family was totally serious all the time. In fact, they were *grim*."

She turned and started to leave. "Straighten up, okay, girls? Better keep this room neat. It's hardly big enough for one person, let alone two twelve-year-old slobs."

"I'm not a slob," Jada said, finally climbing to her feet. She frowned at me. "You can thank me for getting you off the hook with Mom."

I shook my head. "I'm not thanking you for anything," I said bitterly. I picked up Mom's letter from where it had fallen onto the floor.

The doorbell buzzed downstairs. "That must be

Stan," she said. "I'm going over to his house to hang out for a while."

She grabbed her coat and hurried out the door.

I waited until I heard the front door slam. Then I made my way to the telephone on Jada's desk.

I'm going to call Mom, I decided.

I've got to find out what this letter means.

Why did Mom say I'd know the truth by now? Why did she ask me to forgive her? Why did she write as if I'd never see her again?

I sat down in Jada's desk chair. Set the letter down in front of me. Picked up the phone and started to punch in my number.

One ring. Two rings. Three . . . four . . .

I let the phone ring twelve times before I hung up.

I glanced at the clock on Jada's bed table. Mom must have gone out, I realized.

But it's odd. She usually leaves the answering machine on during the day. I guess she forgot.

I clicked off the phone and set it down. I had a fluttery feeling in my chest. My throat suddenly felt very dry.

I smoothed Mom's letter out on the desktop and started to read it again. My eyes slid down the page, catching a phrase here and a phrase there.

"Soon you will learn the truth."

The truth? About what?

"The hardest part is knowing that things will never be the same."

Why does she say that? What is changing?

"Don't forget me."

My eyes stopped at that line. The words repeated

in my head like an endless chant.

Finally, I folded the letter up and tucked it away in my dresser drawer. I didn't want to read it anymore.

I didn't want to read it until I could talk to Mom and find out what she meant.

"Hey—!" I cried out as an idea flashed into my mind.

Beth!

Beth should be home from school. Beth will cheer me up, I decided.

I'll tell her about Jada and how horrible she has been to me. And maybe Beth will have an idea about what Mom was writing about in her letter.

I already began to feel better as I punched Beth's number into the phone. I missed Beth. I really did. I didn't have anyone I could talk to here.

The phone rang three times. Then I heard Beth's familiar voice. "Hello?"

"Beth, hi. It's me!" I said excitedly.

To my surprise, there was a long silence at the other end.

"Beth—it's me," I repeated. "Selena. I'm in Chicago."

"Oh. Hi," she said finally. She sounded very surprised.

"How *are* you?" I asked. "I'm so glad to talk to you. What's up?"

Another long silence. Then she said very softly, "I—I didn't think you'd call."

"Excuse me? What do you mean?" I asked. "I just wanted to talk to you. I haven't seen you since Friday."

"I know," Beth replied, almost in a whisper.

"It's so weird here," I said. "Jada hasn't changed a bit. She's still horrible, Beth. And today she played the meanest trick on me. She—"

"I really can't talk," Beth cut in.

"What? Are you busy or something? I can call back later if you want."

"No!" she said sharply. Then another long silence.

I could hear her breathing. Rapid, shallow breaths.

I suddenly had a heavy feeling in my stomach. "What's wrong, Beth?" I asked.

"I—I can't talk to you, Selena," she said. "I'm really sorry."

Her voice cracked. She sounded about to cry.

"I don't understand!" I cried. "What are you saying?"

I could hear Beth take a deep breath. "They told me I can't talk to you," she said. "They told me we'd both be in danger."

"*Who* told you?" I shouted. "Who? What is this about, Beth? Why can't you talk to me? *Answer* me!"

"Please," she whispered. "Please don't call here again."

I heard a click, and the line went dead.

I sat at Jada's desk, staring at the phone. I don't know how long I sat there.

Beth's tight, trembling voice repeated in my ear. *"Please don't call here again."*

How could Beth say that? She is my best friend!

I picked up the letter. I felt shaky and weird as I made my way down to the kitchen. "Aunt Janet—can I show you something?" I asked.

She was at the stove, dumping dry spaghetti into a pot of boiling water. "I'm trying a spicy new tomato sauce," she said. "Hope you like spicy foods, dear."

"I—I want to show you this letter from my mom," I said.

She dried her hands and took the letter from me. Frowning, she moved her lips as she read. Finally, she handed the letter back to me.

"What does it mean?" I asked in a high, shrill voice.

"Your mother must have been very upset when

45

she wrote this. But I have no idea why." Aunt Janet placed a hand on my shoulder. "My sister always was a moody one. Maybe she was just having one of her bad days. Don't worry too much about it, Selena. The next time I talk to her, I'll find out what she meant. I promise."

After dinner, my aunt and uncle drove to the mall to do some shopping. Jada was downstairs in the living room, watching a show about supermodels on MTV.

I sat at Jada's desk in our bedroom. And pictured Jada as a model, walking down a runway in a short skirt, so tall and skinny, her long legs gleaming in the bright lights, her blond hair flying behind her.

I turned to the phone. I couldn't stop thinking about Mom's letter. My stomach felt knotted and tight. At dinner, I'd barely touched my spaghetti.

"Come on, Mom," I said out loud. "Be there, okay?"

I punched in the number and pressed the phone to my ear.

It rang twice, and then I heard three very loud, very shrill beeps. And a recorded message came on. A woman's voice, speaking very slowly and clearly:

"We're sorry, but the number you are calling is no longer in service."

I clicked the phone off. My hands were suddenly ice cold.

No longer in service? That's impossible.

I realized I must have dialed the wrong number.

I punched it in again, slowly and carefully this time.

Again I heard the three shrill tones. And the same recording: *"We're sorry, but the number you are calling is no longer in service."*

I clicked off the phone again, squeezing it hard in my cold, wet hand. "It has to be a mistake," I told myself.

I had an idea. Aunt Rose. My dad's sister. My aunt was away, but I knew she checked in with my mom every day.

I'll call and leave a message on her answering machine, I decided. She checks her machine all the time. I'll tell Aunt Rose to call me here and let me know what's happening with Mom.

Music from the TV drifted up from downstairs. I heard Jada laugh about something she was watching.

I raised the phone close to my face and pushed Aunt Rose's number. I cleared my throat and rehearsed my message.

The phone rang once. Twice.

And then three shrill beeps rang in my ear. And the same recorded woman's voice came on, speaking so slowly, so clearly:

"We're sorry, but the number you are calling is no longer in service."

Maybe the phone is broken, I thought. That didn't really make sense. But it was the only thing I could think of.

Who else can I call? I asked myself, my mind spinning.

I glanced at the clock. A little after seven. Mom was probably at work or on her way there. I'll call her at the phone company.

I had to get Mom's number from my wallet. I didn't know it by heart, because I never call her at work.

I dialed the number. The phone rang once. Then a taped message began. I groaned as the woman's voice droned on and on. . . . *"If you are calling to add service or upgrade your present service, press three. . . . If you are calling about a repair, press four. . . . "*

After a long while, the voice told me to stay on the line for a service representative. Then I listened to bouncy piano music for nearly ten minutes.

Finally, a woman—a live woman—picked up and

asked if she could help me.

"I—I'd like to speak to my mom," I stammered. "She works there. In the supervisor's office."

"I'll transfer you," the woman said.

I heard several clicks. A silence. Then five more minutes of piano music. "I'm going to go *Craaaazy!*" I exclaimed out loud.

"Can I help you?" a man asked at the other end of the line.

"I'm trying to reach my mother," I replied shrilly. "Alice Miles. Has she come in?"

Silence. Then, "Could you repeat the name, please?"

"Yes. Alice Miles," I said. I spelled Miles for him. "She works in the supervisor's office," I added.

A longer silence. I could hear him typing on a keyboard. "I'm sorry," he said. "I can't find an Alice Miles."

"Huh? But—she has worked there for over ten years!" I cried. "This is CitySouth Bell, right? Main office?"

"Yes, it is," he replied.

"Then she has to be there! Alice Miles."

Another long silence. More keyboard clicking. "I'm sorry, miss," he said finally. "But no one by that name works here."

I felt stunned. As if I'd had the breath knocked out of me.

I gripped the edge of the desk and struggled to breathe.

That man is wrong, I told myself. He made a mistake.

Of *course* Mom works at the phone company.

I decided to try again. I picked up the phone—but it rang in my hand. I was so startled, I dropped it onto the desk.

Fumbling, I picked it up and answered. I hoped it was Mom. But it was Caitlin, a friend of Jada's.

I called downstairs to Jada to pick up the phone. I'll try again as soon as she gets off, I decided.

I waited. And waited. I could hear Jada jabbering on with her friend. She is *never* getting off! I realized.

Sighing, I opened my math textbook. I had almost forgotten that we had a math test the next day.

Maybe this will help me forget about reaching Mom for a while, I thought. I tried to concentrate on the math problems. But it wasn't easy.

Later, it took me hours to fall asleep. I lay covered up to my chin in the twin bed, staring at the ceiling. Thinking about Mom. And Beth. And listening to Jada's steady, shallow breathing in the bed across from mine.

I don't know when I finally fell asleep. But I was awakened by a rustling sound in the center of the room.

I blinked one eye open, then the other. Half awake, I squinted through the darkness at Jada's bed. Empty. The covers had been tossed back. The pillow hung over the side.

For a moment, I thought I was dreaming.

But then I saw a figure moving near the dresser. I was still half asleep, half awake. My eyes wanted to close.

I forced them open. I struggled to focus.

Jada. I realized it was Jada standing across the room in the dark. Staring hard, I could see her pulling a sweater down over her head.

She was getting dressed. Silently. Without turning on any lights.

I turned to the bed table clock. Just past two in the morning.

She had lied about getting a drink of water. She is sneaking out again, I realized. Why? Where would she go at two in the morning?

A tree branch tapped at the windowpane. I could hear the wind howling around the side of the house.

"Jada?" I tried to call out to her. But my voice was clogged from sleep.

I saw her bend to pull on her boots.

Then darkness rolled over me. Heavy and silent.

I guess I fell back to sleep.

I had several strange dreams. Colorful, loud dreams. I remembered someone chasing me. And falling, falling for miles.

The loud buzz of the alarm clock snapped me awake. I sat up, eyes wide open. I shook my head hard, shaking away the memory of the dreams. Then I turned to Jada's bed.

Still empty.

Did she really get dressed in the middle of the night and sneak out of the house? Or was that a dream too?

It had to be a dream—right?

I pulled on a clean pair of straight-legged jeans and an oversize sweater. Then I brushed my hair, put on my shoes, and hurried down the stairs.

I smelled coffee brewing in the kitchen. And I heard my aunt and uncle talking. "That burglary was just two blocks from here," Uncle Will said.

"Wow. And was it the same weird guy?" Aunt Janet asked.

"Yeah. A neighbor saw him. The guy wears a blue cape and mask. Like it's Halloween or something," Uncle Will replied. "And he leaves a little card. With a blue weasel on it."

Aunt Janet laughed. "A blue weasel? This guy is freaky!"

"It isn't funny," my uncle muttered. "He's real dangerous."

I stepped into the kitchen. Uncle Will sat at the table with the newspaper and a mug of coffee. Aunt Janet stood at the sink, sipping from her coffee mug.

And Jada sat across from her father, a bowl of cereal in front of her. "Good morning," all three of them greeted me at once.

"Morning," I muttered.

My aunt poured me a glass of orange juice. As I took my seat, Uncle Will jumped up. "I'm late," he said. He emptied his coffee mug. Then gave us a quick wave and hurried away.

Aunt Janet hurried into the hall, carrying a stack of envelopes for him to mail.

Jada and I were alone in the kitchen. She spooned up cereal with one hand, twisted a strand of her blond hair with the other.

I leaned across the table and whispered, "Where did you go last night?"

She lowered her spoon and glared at me. "Excuse

me? What are you talking about?"

"In the middle of the night," I whispered. "Did you get up?"

"Of course not," she replied sharply. "Are you starting *that* again?"

"I . . . I thought I saw you getting dressed in the dark," I said.

She snickered. "Dream a lot?"

I took a sip of orange juice. "Sorry," I muttered to Jada. "I had a lot of weird dreams last night."

"Face it. You're weird," Jada said. She raised the cereal bowl to her face and slurped down the milk.

A few hours later, Miss Colgate passed out the math tests.

I signed my name at the top. Then I glanced down the page at the math problems. "Whoa," I muttered.

What *was* this stuff? None of it looked familiar.

I raised my hand. "Miss Colgate? Are you sure this is the right test?" I asked.

I heard stirring around the room. A few kids snickered.

Miss Colgate drummed her fingers on her desk-top. "Yes, it's the right test," she replied. "Is there a problem?"

"Well . . . isn't the test on chapters seventeen through twenty?" I asked.

Miss Colgate narrowed her eyes at me. "No,

Selena," she said softly. "We haven't read those chapters yet. Today's test is on chapter nine."

I let out a long sigh. I knew what had happened. Jada.

Jada again. She knew I hadn't been there for the assignment. She deliberately told me the wrong chapters to study.

What am I going to do? I asked myself. I can't let her keep doing this to me.

Why does she hate me so much? There *has* to be a reason.

I failed the test. I didn't know how to work any of the problems.

After class, I hurried out to the hall to catch up to Jada. I grabbed her by the shoulder and spun her around.

"Why do you hate me?" I screamed. "Tell me. Why do you hate me so much?"

I expected her to deny it. I expected her to say "Selena, I don't hate you at all."

But instead, her eyes flashed and her mouth twisted into a cold grin. And she said, "Why do I hate you? You'll find out. Real soon."

Jada went to Stan's house for dinner. Aunt Janet and Uncle Will took me out for Chicago-style pizza. We had a nice time.

I didn't mention the mean trick Jada played on me in math class. And I didn't tell them about Jada's strange answer to my question, even though it stayed in my mind.

I really wanted to solve my problems with Jada without getting my aunt and uncle into it.

I was up in our bedroom, reading the *right* math pages, when Jada returned home. It was a little before ten.

I tried acting normal with her. I was tired, and I really didn't feel like a fight.

"Hi. What's up with Stan?" I asked.

Jada pulled a nightshirt from the dresser and started changing for bed. "Not much," she said. "He got a new CD player."

"Cool," I replied.

"We hooked it up and tried it out," Jada said. She tossed the clothes she had been wearing on the floor beside my bed.

"Where does Stan live?" I asked.

"By the railroad tracks," Jada said. "In a tiny little house. Stan's room is about as big as that closet."

I shook my head. "That's too bad."

"His mother is the *worst* cook," Jada groaned, climbing into bed. "I couldn't believe what she gave us for dinner. I think she made it with dog-food helper."

I laughed. "My mom is even worse," I said. "She's even cheaper. She uses helper helper!"

Jada frowned at me. "Is that supposed to be funny?"

She clicked off the light, even though I wasn't ready for bed.

That's the nicest talk I've had with Jada since I arrived.

My last thought before drifting off to sleep.

Later, I was awakened once again by a rustling sound. I blinked open my eyes and glimpsed Jada climbing out of her bed. She tiptoed across the room.

I glanced at the clock. Two thirty-five.

The tree branch tapped at our window. Pale light washed in from a big half-moon.

In the dim light, I could see my cousin quickly pulling a sweatshirt down over a pair of tights.

So it wasn't a dream, I told myself.

Jada really does get out of bed in the middle of the night and silently gets dressed.

But—then what?

What does she do? Where does she go?

She turned suddenly toward my bed.

I shut my eyes. I didn't want her to know I was watching her.

She stood perfectly still for a moment. Checking to make sure I hadn't woken up. Then she bent down and silently began to pull on her boots.

I'm going to follow her, I decided.

I'm going to solve the mystery. I'm going to find out where she goes at night.

Jada crept out of the bedroom into the dark hall.

As soon as she was out of sight, I jumped out of bed.

I straightened my pajamas as I tiptoed across the room to the bedroom door. "Oh—" I tripped over the pile of clothes Jada had dropped on the floor.

I staggered forward a few steps. Caught my balance.

I froze, listening hard. Had she heard me?

No.

I crept into the hall. I blinked, waiting for my eyes to adjust to the dim light.

I could see Jada moving slowly, carefully, to the end of the hall.

She isn't going to the stairs, I realized. Doesn't

she plan to go downstairs to get outside?

My heart raced. My bare feet were suddenly cold. The cold ran up my body, making me shiver.

I took a few silent steps closer. The floorboard creaked under my feet. A loud *craaack*.

Did Jada hear it?

She stopped with her back to me. For a moment, she stood as still as a statue.

And then she whirled around quickly.

I was caught!

I let out a gasp. Tried to melt into the shadows. And fell back. Into a doorway.

I clapped my hand over my mouth to keep from making a sound. And waited, listening hard.

Did Jada see me?

Silence. Such a heavy silence, I could hear the thudding heartbeats in my chest.

And then I heard Jada's soft footsteps moving away.

Safe. She didn't see me.

Still trembling, I poked my head out from the safety of the doorway. Squinting into the grayness, I saw my cousin step up to the wall at the end of the hall.

What on earth is she doing? I asked myself. And why do I have such a bad feeling about this?

I saw Jada's hand move. She reached up to the bookshelf against the wall. Did she pull out a book? It was too dark to see.

I heard a soft hum. And the bookshelf began to slide.

I blinked several times and tried to focus. I thought maybe the darkness was playing tricks on me.

But no.

The bookcase slid aside. I could see a doorway behind it. A hidden room!

Jada glanced back one more time. Then she vanished into the room.

I heard the soft hum again as the bookshelf slid back into place.

My mind spinning, I crept out into the hall. What was she doing in there? A shiver ran down my body. I hugged myself, staring at the bookshelf.

I had a sudden urge to run up to it. Find the switch. Slide open the shelf and follow Jada into the secret room.

No, I decided.

I don't want another fight with my cousin. She is already so mean to me. She already *hates* me.

I'll wait till she's out of the house, I decided. And then I'll do my exploring.

I'll examine the secret room when Jada isn't around. Maybe I can find out what she is up to without upsetting her. Without having to face her.

Shivering, I took one last glance at the bookshelf. Then I tiptoed back to my room and slid under the covers.

• • •

The next morning, Jada's bed was still empty. I dressed quickly and hurried downstairs.

Jada sat at the breakfast table, running her hands through her unbrushed hair. "Morning," she muttered.

"Morning," I echoed. I slid across from Jada and studied her.

She had dark circles under her eyes. Her hair was a mass of tangles. She yawned loudly.

"What's your problem?" she snapped.

I guess I was staring too hard. I lowered my eyes. "Nothing," I muttered.

I wanted to say, "Where did you go last night? What do you do in the middle of the night?" The words were on the tip of my tongue.

But instead, I reached for the box of cornflakes and began to fill my bowl.

I heard a woman's voice. And realized the kitchen radio was on.

"Another house robbery in Elmwood," the woman was saying. "Witnesses told police they saw a masked figure in a blue cape running through the neighborhood. Police say they have no clues as to the identity of this daring burglar who enters houses in the middle of the night. . . ."

I didn't want to go into that secret room by myself. I had no idea what I would find in there. I wanted someone to come with me.

So after school the next day, I caught up to Stan. He was pulling books from his locker and shoving them into his backpack.

He slammed the locker shut when he saw me coming. "Selena—what's up?"

I glanced around the crowded hall. Kids were laughing and talking, pulling on their coats, getting ready to leave. I glimpsed Jada at the end of the hall, talking to Cindy and a couple of other girls.

I leaned close to Stan and whispered, "Can you help me this afternoon? I'm a little worried about Jada. Can you help me do some spy work?"

He scratched his thick brown hair and narrowed his dark eyes at me. "Spy work? You mean spy on Jada?"

"Not exactly," I replied. "There is something

strange going on at her house. Can you come over there with me?"

He pulled his wool ski cap over his hair. "Isn't Jada going ice-skating with Cindy this afternoon?"

I nodded. "Are you going with them or anything?"

"No," he replied. He waved to some guys across the hall. "I have to go home and walk the dog."

"Think the dog could wait a little while?" I asked. "I know it sounds crazy. But there's a room in the house I have to explore. And I'd really like someone to come help me."

He snickered. "You're scared?"

"No way," I said. "It's just . . . well . . ." I tugged his arm. "Come on. It won't take long. I promise."

We stepped into a cold, gray day. Low clouds floated over the houses and trees, threatening snow. The air felt damp and heavy.

As we walked to Jada's house, I told Stan everything. I told him about Jada getting dressed in the middle of the night. And about the hidden room she disappeared into.

"It's a total mystery," I said.

"Did you ask her about it?" Stan asked.

"Yes, the first time," I replied. "She said she didn't get up. She said I was dreaming. And she was really angry that I asked."

Stan scrunched up his face. I could see he was thinking hard. "Weird," he muttered. "It's too weird."

We reached the house. I pulled out the door key Aunt Janet had given me. We stepped inside. The warm air felt good on my frozen face. "Anyone home?" I called.

I knew my aunt and uncle were at work.

I pulled Stan to the stairs. We didn't stop to take off our coats or backpacks.

I led the way up the stairs, down the hall to the bookcase at the end.

"The room is hidden behind these shelves," I said, whispering even though no one was home. I suddenly felt frightened. I couldn't explain why.

Did I really want to know what was in the secret room?

Stan stared at the bookcase. "Wow! You mean the bookcase moves? How cool! Maybe it's some kind of secret passage!"

I pulled a book from the bottom shelf. Nothing happened. I pulled another book out. "There must be a button to push or something," I said. "It was too dark last night. I couldn't really see what Jada did."

Stan stepped up beside me. We both started lifting books out one at a time.

"Here. I think I found it," I said. I pointed to a small black lever hidden behind a large atlas. I pushed the lever down.

And heard the hum. And watched the bookshelf start to slide to the left.

"Yessss!" I cried, pumping my fist in the air.

Stan's eyes grew wide as a dark wooden door appeared behind the bookcase. "Whoa. This is like a movie or something!" He turned to me. "Are you sure you want to do this?"

"Not really," I answered, my voice trembling. "But I have to. I have to know what Jada is doing at night."

I grabbed the door handle. "Are you coming in with me?"

"Okay," he whispered. "Let's go."

I pulled open the door. The room behind it was totally dark.

I took a step inside and swept my hand over the wall, searching for a light switch.

Stan stepped in behind me. He huddled so close, he bumped into me.

"Okay!" I found the switch and clicked it on. A bulb hanging from the ceiling flashed on.

Blinking against the bright yellow light, I glanced around.

The room was not much bigger than a closet. It was completely bare, no furniture at all. The ratty brown carpet had a long tear in it. The gray paint on the walls was peeling.

A window on the wall across from us was covered by a wide black shade. A single wooden shelf was built into the wall next to the window. It appeared to have something resting on it.

Stan pulled off his ski cap and shoved it into his

coat pocket. His brown hair was matted to his forehead.

"Why would Jada come in *here*?" he asked. "It's just an empty closet."

I shrugged. "Beats me. I'm totally confused. I thought we'd find something really interesting."

I stepped past Stan and crossed to the shelf on the wall. I saw a dark pile of cloth folded neatly on the shelf.

No. Not cloth.

I pulled part of it down and unfolded it. A long blue-black cloak.

I held it out in front of me. "Check this out, Stan. It's like a cape with a hood."

"Weird," he said, studying it. He pulled the rest of the stuff off the shelf. "Look." He held up a pair of black tights. Long, silky black gloves. An oval-shaped blue pendant on a chain. And then a mask. A black mask with two cat-eye holes cut into the front.

"Must be some kind of Halloween costume," he said.

I took the mask from him and rolled it around in my hands. "Why would anyone leave a Halloween costume back here in a hidden room?" I asked.

I slid the mask under the hood of the cloak. And then another idea struck me. "It looks like some kind of superhero costume," I said. *"The Masked Cape Person!"*

Stan still had the black tights in his hand. "Yeah.

69

Well, I guess that's what superheroes wear, right? Tights and a cape?"

I raised the cloak in front of me. "Do you think this is Jada's? Think she wears this stuff?"

Stan shook his head. His face was knotted in confusion.

I laughed. "Maybe Jada has a secret life that no one knows about. Maybe she sneaks in here at night and puts on this costume, and *pretends* to be the Masked Cape Person!"

Stan shook his head. "This is just too weird," he said again.

And then his expression changed. His eyes went wide. He suddenly turned pale. "Selena—" he whispered, staring at the mask in my hand.

"What? What's wrong?" I asked.

"What if—what if that's a *burglar* costume?"

I let out a gasp. "Excuse me?"

"It looks like something a burglar might wear," Stan said. "And didn't they say on the news—"

"That the person who has been robbing houses in Elmwood wore a mask and a cape?" I cut in.

Stan nodded excitedly.

"But that's totally insane!" I cried. "Jada a burglar? That's too stupid, Stan. She's a twelve-year-old girl, like me. She doesn't put on a costume and sneak out in the middle of the night to rob houses."

I moved to the window and tugged on the shade until it slid up. Gray light washed into the room. The window had been left open a crack.

I peered outside. A high tree branch rested right outside. It would be easy for someone to climb out this window onto the tree branch—and then climb down to the ground.

What was I thinking?

"You are *so* not right," I told Stan. "No way my cousin is a burglar!"

Stan nodded. "Yeah. It's a stupid idea. Don't ever tell Jada I said it."

He started to fold up the tights. "I don't think we solved the mystery, Selena."

"We made the mystery even more mysterious," I said. I tugged down the shade. Then I started to fold the cloak.

"Hey—is anybody home?" a voice called.

Stan and I both gasped.

Jada's voice. From downstairs.

We were caught!

Stan and I both dove for the door. We reached it at the same time and bumped each other hard.

I heard Jada's footsteps on the stairs.

"Hurry—go!" I gave Stan a push. Then I stumbled out of the little room behind him.

"Selena—are you home?" Jada called.

"Yes. I'm up here!" I shouted.

I turned to the shelf and pushed the lever up. Would the bookcase slide closed before Jada saw us?

Stan ran down the hall and stopped Jada at the top of the stairs. "Hey—what's up?" he asked. He was trying to sound normal and calm, but his voice cracked.

The bookcase slid shut.

I breathed a sigh of relief and hurried to join them.

"What are *you* doing here?" Jada asked Stan. Her blond hair was a mess, standing up all around her face. Her cheeks were bright red.

"He—he came to see you," I chimed in.

"That's right," Stan agreed. "I forgot you were going ice-skating with Cindy."

"What happened?" I asked. "How come you're home so early?"

"Too windy," Jada replied. She tried to brush down her hair with both hands. "Too windy and too cold. We're going to try again Saturday afternoon."

She and Stan disappeared downstairs. I went into the bedroom and started up the computer.

The night before, I had emailed Mom and Aunt Rose. I wrote that I couldn't reach them on the phone. I pleaded with them to call me as soon as possible. I emailed Beth too, asking her why she had acted so weird.

Now I stared at the monitor screen. All three messages had been returned. *Undeliverable,* the computer said.

"What is going on?" I cried. I could feel tears brimming behind my eyes.

I picked up the phone and called Information. I asked for my mom's number. I was desperate. It couldn't be disconnected. It couldn't!

The operator said the listing had been removed. I made her check three times.

Removed.

I can't take this, I thought. I can't take this anymore. This is *Crazy!*

I was frantic to talk to my aunt and uncle. But

they didn't come home. Jada told me Aunt Janet had called to say that she and Uncle Will were having dinner in town and going to a movie.

Jada and I shared a frozen pizza. She talked to friends on the phone as we ate. She didn't say a word to me. Then she disappeared to her room.

Later, I watched a sitcom on TV for a while, a rerun of *Sabrina*. Anything to take my mind off things. But I couldn't concentrate on it.

Go upstairs and ask Jada about the secret room! I ordered myself. *Just do it!*

I took a deep breath. All day, I had been practicing what I'd say. But I ran through it in my mind one more time:

"Jada, I don't want you to think I'm a horrible snoop or anything. But I found out about the secret room. And I saw the costume inside. I'm really sorry if it's a big secret. But I have to know. What is it all about?"

With those words repeating in my head, I pulled myself up the stairs. And stepped into our room.

"Jada, I have to talk to you," I said.

"Jada?"

She was gone.

I stood in the doorway, my eyes searching the room. The beds were unmade. The computer had been left on. A pile of Jada's clothes blocked the door to the closet.

I stepped back into the hall. "Jada? Are you up here?" I shouted.

No reply.

She didn't say she was going out. And I hadn't heard her leave the house.

"Jada?"

I trotted down the hall to the bookcase. I put my ear against it and listened. No sound from the tiny room.

I hurried back downstairs. Checked the living room. Then made my way to the kitchen.

No sign of her.

I cupped my hands around my mouth and called one more time.

No. Jada had left.

"Weird," I muttered. I pulled a Coke from the fridge and returned to my chair in front of the TV. The show clattered on, lots of shouting voices and loud audience laughter.

It was all a blur to me.

I don't know how much time passed. Finally, I realized I had to snap myself out of my daze. "Maybe I'll read a book," I decided.

I clicked off the TV and climbed out of my chair. I started up the stairs to find a book—when the phone rang.

I darted into our room and picked up the phone. "Hello?"

"Selena? Oh, thank goodness!" Jada's voice at the other end. But she sounded so strange.

"Jada? What's wrong?" I asked, pressing the phone to my ear.

"I—I can't answer any questions," she replied. "I'm desperate. You've just got to listen to me!"

"Okay, okay," I murmured. My heart started to thud. "Go ahead."

"I have only a second, Selena," she whispered. "They—they're coming back."

"Who?" I cried. "Jada—are you in trouble?"

"I can't explain." She was whispering so low, I could barely hear her. "I'm in terrible trouble. I'm being held prisoner."

"*What?*" I shrieked.

"You've got to hurry," Jada whispered. "You're the only one who can help. *Listen to me!*"

My throat was suddenly so dry, I couldn't swallow. "I am," I choked out. "I'm listening."

"Upstairs," Jada said. "There's a secret room. At the end of the hall. It's hidden behind the bookshelf."

I don't believe it! I thought. She's telling me about the hidden room.

But why?

"There's a lever behind the big atlas," she continued breathlessly. "Pull the book out, and you'll see it."

"Okay," I said. "Then what?"

"The shelf will slide open. Go inside the room. Can you hear me?"

"Yes. Just barely," I replied.

"I have to whisper," she said. "I can't let them hear me. They're so dangerous. I—I don't know what they plan to do with me."

"Who?" I cried. "Who is it?"

"Listen. Go into the room," Jada continued. "You'll see a costume on a shelf. Put it on."

"Huh?" I cried.

"Please—don't ask questions. They're coming back any second," Jada whispered. "Put on the costume. The mask and everything. Put it on and hurry over here as fast as you can."

She whispered an address.

My mind was spinning. I felt dizzy and sick.

"But how can I help?" I asked. "How can I rescue you?"

"Just walk into the house, Selena. When they see you in the costume, they'll run. Trust me. You can do this. Just hurry."

Jada gasped. "I hear them coming back. *Hurry!* I'm so scared!"

I stood for a long while with the phone still pressed against my ear, staring at the wall. Then I dropped the phone to the desk.

I'm not going to fall for this, I decided.

I've fallen for every one of Jada's tricks. But not this time.

I know what this is about. She wants me to put on the costume and come running over to one of her friend's houses. When I come bursting in, they'll all have a big laugh at the geek in the stupid costume.

Well . . . no way. No way, Jada. How dumb do you think I am?

I gazed down at the phone. Once again I heard Jada's whispered voice in my ear. So terrified. So desperate.

I shuddered. Was Jada that good an actress?

She really did sound scared.

What if this was real? What if it wasn't a joke?

Jada had been sneaking out in the middle of the

night. What if she had gotten herself into some major trouble?

"Maybe Jada was telling the truth," I told myself.

Yes. There was a chance that she really was being held prisoner. And that she was counting on me to rescue her. A chance that I was her last hope.

I have to follow her instructions, I decided. I can't let something awful happen to Jada just because I didn't believe her.

My legs felt as wobbly as Jell-O. But I forced myself down the hall to the bookcase. I tugged the big atlas off the shelf. It fell from my trembling hands and thudded to the floor.

I didn't bother to pick it up. I pressed the lever down. Heard the hum start up—and watched the bookshelf slide away.

I didn't wait for it to move all the way. I pulled open the hidden door and burst into the tiny room.

My hand fumbled for the light switch. I found it and clicked on the light.

"Hurry, Selena. Hurry," I urged myself on.

I grabbed the costume off the shelf. The black tights fell to the floor. I picked them up and started to pull them on.

No. Oh, no. They're not going to fit, I realized.

These are Jada's, and she's six inches taller than me, and so skinny.

I tugged them up. They were twisted, and I had to turn them as I pulled. To my surprise, they fit perfectly.

I grabbed the cloak and slid it over my shoulders. My hands were trembling so hard, it took me four tries to fasten the laces around my throat.

Hurry. Hurry.

The oval pendant was heavier than I'd imagined. I slid the chain over my head and pulled the pendant into place.

The silky black mask slid from my hands. I picked it up and turned it until I found the front.

The eye holes were cut so narrow, shaped like cat eyes. Would I be able to see?

I tugged the mask down over my face. I struggled to adjust it over my hair. Then I twisted it until the eye holes were in front of my eyes.

The long black gloves were still on the shelf. I pulled them down and started to slide one on.

They're probably way too small, I thought. Jada has such tiny, slender hands.

But to my surprise, the gloves also fit perfectly.

Done. The costume was complete.

There was no mirror in the little room. So I couldn't see how I looked. But it didn't matter. Jada's whispered words repeated in my ear.

"Just walk into the house, Selena. When they see you in the costume, they'll run."

I pushed the long cape behind me and ran out of the hidden room. I pressed the lever, sliding the bookcase back into place.

I tore through the hall, then down the stairs. The

TV was still on in the living room. I pulled open the front door and leaped out.

A dark, moonless night. The cold air hit my face as I started to run to the street. Trees swayed in the strong gusts. A few doors down, I heard a baby crying. The lights went off in the house across the street.

Dead leaves crackled under my thudding boots. I stayed along the hedges, in the shadows, away from the street. I didn't want anyone to see me in this weird costume.

What would they think?

I was breathing noisily, wheezing as I ran. I struggled to force back my panic. But I'd never been so terrified in all my life.

Who was holding Jada prisoner? Why did Jada think this costume would scare them away?

A thousand questions flew through my head, all of them frightening. I knew I wouldn't have answers to any of them until Jada was rescued.

Rescued . . .

Rescued . . .

What if I didn't get there in time?

The address Jada had whispered was a few blocks from the ice-skating pond.

I reached the house and stopped at the curb. I grabbed onto the mailbox. Held on to it with both hands as if it were a life preserver.

Leaning on it, I struggled to catch my breath. Struggled to slow my racing heartbeats. And waited for my legs to stop throbbing.

Finally, I let go and stared across the small front lawn at the house. A low, ranch-style house. Completely dark. No lights anywhere.

No car in the driveway. No sign of life.

Could this be the right house? I squinted at the address on the mailbox.

Yes.

I started up the lawn. My long cape swirled behind me in the wind. It tangled around my legs, and I had to pull it loose.

My face was sweating under the mask. The mask made my cheeks itch. It stuck to my forehead.

I sucked in deep breaths, one after another. Forced my legs to move.

I stepped up to the front door.

Silence inside. The wind whispered behind me. Trees creaked and groaned.

My hand went up to push the bell. But I stopped myself in time.

I grabbed the doorknob. Inside the glove, my hand was wet and colder than the metal.

Was the door locked? I turned the knob. And pushed.

The door slid open silently.

I stared into more darkness. Blacker than the night.

Still not a sound.

I held my breath. Forced one leg forward. Then the other.

I stepped into the dark house. Warm inside.

I waited for my eyes to adjust. But I couldn't see a thing.

Pulling the cloak around me, I took a trembling step. Another.

Another.

Into a dark hallway. My boots thudded heavily on the wooden floor. The only other sound was the shallow wheezing of my breaths.

I stepped into a room, darker and warmer. My eyes squinted into the blackness.

Jada, where are you? I asked silently. *Are you here? Is* anyone *here?*

A terrifying thought made me gasp: What if I'm too late?

I bumped into something hard. A table?

I heard a clattering sound. Scraping footsteps.

The ceiling light flashed on.

"Oh—!" I cried out as someone moved quickly toward me.

A figure in a bright red costume. A red mask over the face. A red cape, tight-fitting red tights and top.

I staggered back. "Who—who are you?" I cried.

"Shadow Girl, don't you recognize me?" she sneered. "I'm Red Raven. I'm your arch-enemy!"

23

I backed into the wall. I stared in shock as the red-caped figure moved toward me. I recognized her voice at once.

"Jada—why are you in that costume?" I demanded angrily. "I don't believe this! Is this another one of your mean tricks?"

She stopped and swung the cape behind her. "It's not a joke," she replied softly. Behind the red mask, her blue eyes lit up like jewels. "I'm not Jada when I wear this costume. I'm Red Raven. And you—"

"Stop it!" I shouted. "Give me a break. Why did you make me put on your other costume? Why did you make me come here?"

"It's not my costume," Jada replied sharply. "Can't you figure it out, Selena? Look at the pendant."

"Huh?" I lifted the oval pendant from my throat.

"Go ahead. Look at it carefully," Jada urged.

Squinting through the eye holes of the mask, I

studied the oval pendant. I saw a face inside the glass. A photograph.

My face.

"It's not my costume," Jada said, hands on her waist. "It's yours. Didn't you wonder why it fit so well?"

I swallowed hard. "Well . . . "

"It's your costume, Selena," Jada said. "It has always been here, waiting for you."

"But—" I started.

Jada's blue eyes flashed again. "And I really am your arch-enemy."

I leaped across the room. And grabbed my cousin by the shoulders. "But that's crazy!" I screamed. "Arch-enemy? What are you *saying*? We live in the real world. We don't live in a comic book!"

She brushed my hands away. "There are all kinds of worlds in the real world," she said softly. "Most people don't know that."

My head was throbbing. I stared at my cousin, trying to make sense of what she was saying.

"Don't try to fight it, Selena," Jada said. "This is your fate. This is what you were born to do."

I saw sadness in Jada's eyes. Or was it anger? "No! I—I don't like this," I stammered.

She sighed. "Now maybe you understand why I have always been so jealous of you."

My mouth dropped open. "Jealous?"

Her voice broke. "Why do you think I've always

been so mean to you? Why do you think I played all those awful jokes to embarrass you?"

"You're . . . jealous?" I repeated.

Jada sighed. "I wish that costume were mine. I'd give anything—*anything*—to be Shadow Girl. But that's not my fate. Not my job."

"Shadow Girl?" I repeated. "What are you talking about?"

"My job is to toughen you up," Jada continued. "To harden you. To test you. To make you angry. To prepare you to be Shadow Girl. And then . . . to destroy you!"

"No!" I cried. "You're crazy! You need help! You're totally nuts!"

I pulled off the black mask and heaved it at her. "I won't do this! I won't! This is a joke! A stupid joke! I want to talk to my mother! I want to see her! I want to see her right away!"

Jada picked up the mask and began to fold it between her hands. "You can't fight your fate," she said softly.

"No! This doesn't make any sense!" I screamed. "I'm twelve years old. I'm not a superhero!"

Jada sighed. She placed a hand on my trembling shoulder. "I wish I could help you," she whispered. "But it is your destiny."

"No—" I wailed. "I hate fighting! I hate super-heroes! I don't believe any of this! It can't be true! It can't!"

"Calm down, Shadow Girl," a voice said from the doorway behind me. "You have to toss away your old life and accept the new."

I spun around. "Aunt Janet!" I cried. "What are *you* doing here?"

"This is our special hideout," Aunt Janet said, closing the door behind her. She wore a long black coat over black leggings. Her dark eyes sparkled in the dim light. "Your uncle Will doesn't know anything about this part of our lives."

I gaped at her. "You too?"

She nodded. "I was the Gray Avenger—until I retired."

My aunt stepped to the far wall and pulled open a cabinet door. She lifted out a large book, bigger than an encyclopedia. The cover was black leather. It appeared to be heavy. She had to hold it in both hands.

"We couldn't reveal anything to you until tonight—a night without a moon. The night of shadows. So it is written in the *Book of Fates*. Has Red Raven told you about the book?" Aunt Janet asked.

"Not yet," Jada said. "Selena has been fighting me. She refuses to understand—"

"This is all insane!" I blurted out.

Holding it in two hands, Aunt Janet raised the book in front of her. And as she lifted it, it began to glow. A yellow-red glow, like fire.

"It isn't crazy, Selena," she said softly. "This is the *Book of Fates*. Your future is written in this book."

I stared at the glowing book as if hypnotized. Bright yellow and red sparks flew off the cover and circled my aunt until she glowed too.

I couldn't believe what I was seeing. Could all this really be true?

"I—I don't understand," I murmured.

Jada pulled two folding chairs from against the wall. Pushing her cape aside, she sat in one of them. She motioned for me to take the other.

Aunt Janet stood in front of us, glowing in the light of the huge book in her hands.

"We come from another world," she said in a whisper. "Our fate is different from those we live with. We have a job—to protect the innocent. To protect people who don't even know we exist."

"But my mom—" I blurted out.

"Your mom had to cut herself off from you," Aunt Janet said. "She cannot be involved. The *Book of Fates* decreed it. Your mother cannot be involved in your training. Your friends had to be instructed to stay away too."

I swallowed. "You mean Beth—?"

Aunt Janet nodded. "Your future is to become

Shadow Girl. It is written in the *Book of Fates*. But you must discover your own powers. You must test yourself and discover your own courage."

Jada snickered. *"What* courage?" she muttered. "She's a total wimp."

"It will take time," Aunt Janet said softly. The sparks flew around her. "We have tested you, Shadow Girl. So far, you have not done well."

"Tested me?" I asked. "You mean—"

"Cindy," Jada said. "Her story about being robbed—it was a fake. You were supposed to show some courage. Instead, you turned green and nearly lost your lunch."

I jumped to my feet. "But—I don't want to do this!" I cried. "I'm not brave. I—I—I don't *want* to do what it says in that book!"

Aunt Janet raised the glowing book higher. "You cannot go against the *Book of Fates*," she said. "Even if it is not what you would choose."

Jada jumped up too and spun me around to face her. "I didn't choose to be Red Raven!" she cried. "It was decreed in the book. My whole life, I wanted to be Shadow Girl. I didn't choose to be your enemy—but I am!"

Aunt Janet let out a long sigh. She returned the book to the cabinet. The room grew darker.

"Yes, our family is now divided," she said sadly. "Shadow Girl and Red Raven are enemies forever." Her voice broke. She turned away. "So unfair. So unfair . . . But we have no choice. We must obey the book."

She strode quickly to the door.

"Aunt Janet?" I started toward her. But Jada pulled me back.

"Use your powers well, Shadow Girl," my aunt whispered. She vanished into the darkness.

"But—but—" I called after her.

Jada gripped my arm hard. "She can't talk about it. She's too upset."

"About you and me?" I asked.

Jada nodded. "Mom couldn't tell you the rest of the story," Jada said. "She's too upset to finish it."

I locked my eyes on Jada's. "What's the rest of the story?" I demanded.

She stared back at me for a moment. Then she said, "It is written in the *Book of Fates* that you will *kill* me!"

"Nooooooo!" A cry escaped my throat.

I pushed past Jada and tore out of the room. I had to get away from her. Away from this house.

My head felt about to split open. Jada's frightening words repeated in my brain until they were a crazy jumble.

I ran through the streets, the cape fluttering behind me. I wish I could fly away from here, I thought. I wish I could fly away and never see these crazy people again.

"Whoooooa!" I let out a startled cry as my feet left the ground—and I took off. The cold wind blew against my face as I flew above the street.

"Oh, wow! They told the truth!" I exclaimed. "I—I have powers! I'm flying!"

I gazed up at the stars and soared higher. The icy air stung my cheeks, but I didn't care. This was incredible!

My cape stretched out behind me, billowing in

the wind, lifting me higher still. I was afraid to look down. Afraid that I would tumble from the sky if I did. But I slowly lowered my eyes and gazed at the streets below. At the houses that dotted them in a perfect pattern. Everything appeared so unreal from up here. So amazing!

I turned and flew over Jada's school, and a few seconds later, I landed in Jada's front yard. "Ow!" I cried out in pain as I dropped to the hard ground on my elbows and knees. My heart pounding, I scrambled into the house.

I sneaked upstairs. My whole body shook. I had to get out of that costume. I stuffed it into the secret room. And changed into jeans and a sweater.

I had to talk to someone. But who? I knew I couldn't reach Mom. And I couldn't call Beth.

I needed a friend. But I didn't have any friends in this new town.

Then it hit me—Stan. Maybe I could talk to him! Maybe he'll have an idea about what I should do.

I looked up his address in the phone book. Then I grabbed my coat and ran out the front door.

It was late. Most of the houses on the block were dark. The air felt heavy and wet. No moon or stars above.

As I neared Stan's house, the neighborhood changed. The houses were run-down and closer together. Front yards were patchy, cluttered with litter and junk.

In an empty lot, I saw three or four men huddled around a trash-can fire. Across the street, a car had been stripped of its tires, the top slashed open.

"Hey, girl—" someone shouted from behind me. "Got any change? How about a dollar?"

I didn't turn back. I started to jog, pulling my coat closer around me.

Maybe this was a mistake, I thought. Stan's neighborhood is really scary at night.

I finally found his house, a small square, dark-shingled house next to an empty lot. Railroad tracks crossed the street at the corner. A two-pump gas station—closed for the night—stood across the street.

I knocked softly on the front door, afraid his parents might be asleep. After a few seconds, Stan pulled the door open. His eyes bulged with surprise. "Selena?"

"Hi. You busy?" I asked.

He pulled the door open wider. I stepped inside. The air was hot and smelled of stale bacon. The wallpaper was dark and had a big stain on one wall.

"I was setting up a new computer," Stan said. "Come this way. My room is in back."

I stepped over a hole in the carpet and followed him to the back of the house. "Are your parents home?" I asked, peeking into the tiny, dark kitchen.

"No. Dad has two jobs," Stan replied. "So we never see him much. And Mom works the late shift at the box factory."

"My mom works nights too," I said.

At least, I *thought* she did. I suddenly wanted to see her so badly. I had to hold back a sob.

Would I ever see her again?

Stan's room was long and narrow. Rock music posters were tacked over one wall. He had a computer on his desk, surrounded by a dozen cables.

He motioned for me to sit down. "What's up?" He stood over his desk, hooking up the monitor.

"I don't know," I said, sighing. "It's been such a weird night."

He picked up the computer mouse. "Now, where do you think you attach this?" He scratched his head.

Does Stan know about Jada's secret identity? I wondered. Does he know any of this superhero stuff?

The other day, when we explored the secret room together, he didn't seem to know anything about the Shadow Girl costume.

I had to find out what he knew. "You know that black costume we found in the hidden room?" I started. "I've been thinking about it. Did Jada wear it last Halloween?"

He scrunched up his face, thinking hard. "No. I think she was a witch last year. Yeah. With a big green wart on her nose." He chuckled.

He doesn't seem to know anything at all about Shadow Girl, I decided. "Do you ever read comic books?" I asked.

He shook his head. "I know Jada is into them. But I never was. Even when I was little."

I can't talk to him about Shadow Girl, I decided. Jada hasn't told him anything. And it's probably supposed to be a secret.

I came all this way because I needed someone to talk to. And I can't talk to Stan.

I suddenly felt totally alone. Totally alone in the world.

Stan pushed the mouse cable into a connection. "Yesss! Victory!"

He stood up, smiling. "Hey, Selena, did Jada tell you about the party Saturday night?"

"Party?"

He nodded. "She probably forgot. She is having a party at her neighbors' house across the street. The Carvers are away all weekend. And they gave Jada the key to their house to take in the mail."

"And so Jada is throwing a party in their house?" I asked. "That's terrible!"

Stan laughed. "The Carvers will never know. We'll clean up everything before they come home."

I frowned at him. "But why is Jada doing it?"

He shrugged. "Why not? Because it's cool."

I climbed to my feet and pulled on my coat. "I'd better get going," I said. "If my aunt and uncle knew I was out this late, they'd have a cow!"

"Guess I'll see you at the party Saturday," Stan said, following me to the front door.

I rolled my eyes. "Yeah. If my dear cousin invites me!"

I said good night and stepped back into the cold, damp night. I felt icy sprinkles on my head, so I pulled up my hood.

I took a few steps along the sidewalk. A garbage can had overturned, spilling a mound of garbage over the sidewalk and street.

I jumped over it and started to walk quickly away.

I had gone less than half a block, when I heard a shrill, high scream behind me. A scream of pure terror.

A chill of fear ran through my body.

I spun around.

And heard another cry. From the darkened gas station across the street.

Through the misty rain, I saw four or five boys. At first I thought they had formed a huddle. Like a football huddle.

But then I realized they had another boy in the middle. A boy in a striped ski cap. The boy who was screaming.

I took a few timid steps closer.

The boys were dressed in black leather and denim.

Squinting through the mist, I saw their arms swing.

Heard the *thud* of fists.

The boy in the ski cap screamed again. A cry of pain.

The others kept him surrounded. Punching. Swinging their arms hard. Grunting loudly with each thrust of a fist.

I watched helplessly as the boy sank to his knees on the wet pavement.

As soon as he dropped, they swooped down on him. They grabbed him by the arms and started to pull him behind the gas station.

My heart hammered in my chest. I felt sick. I pressed my hand against my mouth and glanced around frantically, searching for a policeman. For anyone who could help.

But the street was empty.

"Hey—stop!" I called out. "Leave him alone!"

I didn't think. I didn't plan to shout at them. The words burst from my throat.

Two of the boys turned away from their victim. Pointing at me, they started to run.

"Get her!" one of them yelled.

And then all four of them were tearing after me, running hard, leather jackets flying behind them, shoes stomping the pavement.

Why did I do that? I asked myself.

Did I really think I was some kind of superhero?

My panic froze me in place. I was going to get pounded like that boy.

"You're in trouble now!" a hoarse voice cried.

I sucked in a deep breath. Wheeled around. Forced my legs to move.

"Ohh!" I cried out as I ran straight into a metal trash can.

The can clattered onto its side with me on top of it.

I hit the pavement hard. Tried to roll away so that I could climb back to my feet.

Too late. Too late.

Running hard, swinging their arms, the grinning boys closed in on me.

On my stomach, scrambling to stand up, I slid in the disgusting garbage.

I turned when I heard the squeal of tires. A black SUV came wheeling around the corner.

The driver must not have seen me down on the ground. The big car roared by, inches from my outstretched arms.

Gasping in fright, I struggled to my feet.

And stared at the empty street.

The four boys had vanished. The squealing SUV must have scared them off.

Were they still nearby? Were they watching me? I wasn't going to take that chance.

I pulled my hood back over my head and started to run home. With every step I took, I grew angrier.

Those creeps. Did they think they could beat up anyone they wanted?

Well, I'm not going to let them get away with it, I decided.

Aunt Janet's words echoed in my head: *"Use your powers well, Shadow Girl."*

The costume. I needed the costume.

I didn't know what powers it held. I knew only that without it, I was helpless.

The freezing rain started to come down harder. I ran back to Jada's house, my shoes splashing up puddles on the slick pavement.

Uncle Will's car was in the driveway. I crept silently into the house and upstairs to the bedroom. Jada was asleep with the lights on, lying on her side, her mouth open slightly.

I made my way silently down the hall. Into the secret room. A few seconds later, I was pulling the cloak around me, sliding the pendant around my neck, tugging the mask over my face.

I stopped on my way out the secret door. *Am I really doing this?* I asked myself. *Am I really going out as Shadow Girl?*

I felt excited and terrified at the same time.

I hurried back outside. The cold rain had stopped, but a thick mist hung over the streets.

I turned and began to trot toward Stan's neighborhood. As I moved through the dark, silent streets, I realized I didn't know anything about my powers.

I knew I could fly. But I didn't exactly know how.

Am I super strong? I wondered. *Does the cloak make me invulnerable?*

I stopped in the middle of the street. My breath

puffed up in front of me in little clouds. Beneath the cloak, my whole body was trembling. I've never been this terrified in my whole life, I thought.

Too late to turn back. Too late . . .

The gas station stood just ahead of me. Pushing the cape behind me, I leaned into the wind and ran up to it.

I saw the striped ski cap lying beside a gas pump. I picked it up. And then I saw the boy, still on his back, on the pavement beside the side wall.

As I knelt beside him, he groaned and opened his eyes.

His dark hair was wet and matted to his forehead. He had a deep cut in one cheek, and dark blood had caked under his nose.

He groaned again, holding his side. He blinked several times. When he finally focused his eyes on me, he gasped in fright.

I leaned over him. I brushed back his hair with my glove. "Don't be afraid," I said softly. "I'm your friend. I'm Shadow Girl."

The words sounded so funny to me. So strange. As if another person were saying them.

He squinted at me. "My ribs . . ." he moaned.

"Can you stand up?" I asked. "Should I call for an ambulance? Or call your parents?"

"I—I think I can stand," he said, gently touching his cut cheek. He started to stand. I grabbed his arm and helped pull him up.

"That costume," he said. "Why—"

"Never mind," I said. "I just came back to help you." I handed him his cap. "Who were those guys who beat you up?" I asked.

"*Who wants to know?*" a harsh voice behind me demanded.

Startled, I twisted around—and saw the four tough-looking boys in black leather jackets.

I saw the baseball bats in their hands. I saw their eyes narrow menacingly. Their bodies tensed, as if getting ready for battle.

And then, raising their bats, they moved in on me.

28

A wave of fear swept over me. I can't do this, I thought. I can't fight these boys.

I forced myself to my feet. I took a step toward them. Then another. My cape billowed behind me. The mask clung wetly to my face.

Baseball bats raised in front of them, the four boys circled me.

"You're a little late for Halloween," one of them shouted.

The others laughed.

"Put down those bats," I told them, trying to keep my voice steady. "I'm Shadow Girl. You can't hurt me."

They laughed again. "She's crazy," one of them muttered.

"She's toast," another one said.

My breath caught in my throat. I'm going to get killed! I realized.

How do I fight these creeps?

Please—please—let me be strong! I silently prayed.

They moved in closer, circling, circling. And then a tall boy with cold gray eyes and a silver ring in the side of his nose swung his bat.

He swung it at my waist.

I danced back. Felt the swoosh of cold air as the bat missed me by an inch or two.

The next boy swung his bat at my head. I ducked. Reached out. Grabbed his bat.

I pulled it easily out of his hands. His eyes went wide. I could see he was startled by my strength.

I heaved the bat into the wall of the gas station. It made a loud *clang* and bounced away.

With a grunt, the first boy swung again. I raised my hand. Caught the bat in mid-swing. Tugged it out of his grasp.

And snapped the bat in two between my hands.

"Whoa!"

"Hey—!"

"Weird!"

I could see the surprise on their faces. Surprise—and fear.

I lurched forward. Grabbed the bat from another boy.

He held on to it tightly. Struggled to pull it away from me.

I heaved the bat with all my strength—and watched as the boy and the bat sailed up to the gas station roof.

The boy landed hard. I heard him utter a groan. The bat clattered across the roof.

And then the other three boys took off. Screaming as they ran, they vanished around the front of the gas station and disappeared down the street.

Dizzy, wheezing with every breath, I wheeled around. And saw that the boy with the ski cap had disappeared too.

I stood up straight. A smile spread across my face. "My first victory," I murmured. "I did it! I'm Shadow Girl!"

Then my body shook so hard, I dropped to my knees.

I was sick. Sicker than I'd ever felt in my life.

I bent over and puked my guts out.

I couldn't stop trembling.

Chill after chill ran down my body.

Finally, I felt strong enough to stand up. I wrapped the cloak around me and began to make my way home.

I can't do this, I decided.

I can't be a superhero.

It's not just that I'm scared. I hate it. *Hate* it. *Hate* it!

Back in the bedroom, I woke Jada up. "I can't do this," I said. "I'm sorry. I tried it, and I can't do it."

She blinked up at me through sleep-filled eyes. "What makes you think you have a choice?" she whispered.

· · ·

The next night, Jada forced me to test my powers.

She pulled me to the hidden room. "Hurry. Get dressed. Go," she ordered.

I swallowed hard. "Are you coming with me?"

She shook her head. "I'm your enemy—remember? You must find your own way."

"But—I don't—"

She shoved me into the secret room. "You're so pitiful, Selena, I'll give you one hint," she said. "The power is in the pendant."

"Huh? What does that mean?" I demanded.

She shut the door behind me. I heard the hum of the bookcase as it slid shut.

Hey—I'm locked in here, I thought. But then I remembered the window.

Before I pulled on the costume, I studied the pendant carefully. My photo stared out at me through the dark glass.

Why did Jada say the power was in the pendant?

I squeezed the cool glass between my fingers. I expected it to give off a burst of heat or a flash of light. But nothing happened.

With a sigh, I lowered the pendant around my throat. Then I pulled on the rest of the costume.

I raised the shade and tugged open the window. A blast of cold night air greeted me. I edged off the windowsill onto the tree branch.

Don't look down, Selena, I warned myself. I really

have a problem with heights.

I started to make my way down the fat trunk. "Ow!" I cried out as I scraped my hand on a patch of rough bark.

Not a good start.

I landed hard on the ground, twisting my ankle. Pain throbbed up my leg. I gazed at the back door. I wanted to go back inside and forget this superhero craziness.

But I knew Jada would never let me.

The wind swirled my cape around me. I straightened the mask so that I could see better. Then I made my way to the empty lot at the corner.

The lot was cluttered with rocks and fallen tree limbs.

I'll save the flying for last, I decided. I already know I can fly. The question is, how do I do it?

I decided to test my strength first. I remembered the amazing strength I had when I fought those four boys.

Would I always be that powerful when I wore the Shadow Girl costume?

The moon drifted behind the clouds. A heavy darkness rolled over the empty lot.

I bent down to lift a large, round rock from between a tuft of weeds. "Oh." I strained with both hands, but I couldn't budge the rock.

I decided to try a smaller one. This one was jagged and sharp. Gripping it in two hands, I raised it waist-high. And heaved it.

It plopped to the ground a foot in front of me.

What happened to my amazing strength? I wondered.

Jada's words repeated in my mind: *"The power is in the pendant."*

I picked up a small rock in one gloved hand. And squeezed the pendant with the other. Then I tossed the rock as hard as I could.

It sailed a short distance, then dropped into a clump of tall weeds.

"This is not working," I said out loud.

Maybe I have super speed, I thought. I kicked a clump of dirt out of the way. Then I took off, running across the lot.

I didn't get far. My twisted ankle hurt. And the cape tangled itself around a fallen tree limb.

What am I doing wrong? I wondered. The costume let me fly home. And it worked perfectly against those four creeps at the gas station.

I tried a few more times. I turned and stared hard at the house across the street. No. I didn't have X-ray vision.

I leaned all my weight against a telephone pole at the curb. No. I couldn't make it tilt.

"Use your powers well," Aunt Janet had said.

That meant that I had powers. Why had they vanished tonight? What was I doing wrong?

I glimpsed a white church on the corner of the

next block. It stood high on a hill overlooking the street. Beside the church, the pointed steeple rose up into the black night sky.

"I can fly. I know I can," I said out loud.

Sweeping the cape behind me, I hurried across the street. The back door to the church was open. I climbed the narrow, curving stairs to the top of the steeple.

It opened onto a small deck. I stepped outside. The wind blew so hard, it made the steeple tremble. I looked out on the trees and houses sloping down the block.

My legs were shaking so hard, I could barely stand. My stomach lurched. I started to feel really sick.

Can I fly again? Can I? I have no choice. I have to try it.

I did it once. I can do it again!

A blast of wind made my cape billow behind me. I stepped up to the edge.

I can do it, I decided. I know I can!

I raised my arms above my head. Leaped off the edge of the deck.

And fell straight down . . . down . . . down . . .

I shut my eyes. And prayed: *Please—please—let me fly!*

I waited for the explosion of pain as I hit the ground.

But I felt a tug. Felt myself suddenly pull up.

Opening my eyes, I saw the ground sweep beneath me. *Beneath* me!

I stretched my arms out—and swooped higher. The cold wind rushed against my face, fluttering my mask, blowing the cape behind me like a giant flag.

"Yes! I'm flying again!" I screamed.

Higher, into the black sky. I could see the church and its steeple far below me now. And the cars parked along the street, small as toys.

I was flying—and I knew the secret. The secret of the pendant and its powers.

I had to *wish* for the power first. And when I wished for it, it was given to me.

Yes. I remembered wishing for strength when

those four boys were moving in on me. And I had it.

And now I had wished to fly—and I was soaring over Elmwood, swooping low to the ground, then sailing high over the houses.

How do I keep from crashing into the ground? I wondered. That first landing was really painful. Do I *wish* for a soft landing?

I lowered my arms. I began to sail down. My cape flapped above me. The houses and trees roared up to meet me.

"Noooooooooo!" I wailed. Out of control. I knew I was out of control.

"Ow!" I landed hard on both feet. My legs folded, and I dropped to the wet grass in a sitting position. The cape fluttered down over my head, covering me.

Wow! That was incredible! I thought.

That was awesome!

If I practice and get really good at it . . .

Whoa!

What was I saying? I don't want to do this, I reminded myself. Sure, it was *amazing* to fly through the sky. It was thrilling. But no . . . no way I wanted to spend my life flying after criminals!

What else can I do? I wondered. What other powers do I have?

I pulled myself shakily to my feet. I picked up a rock from the curb. And silently wished for amazing strength.

I heaved the rock—and watched it sail over the

houses, down the block, into the next block.

Yes. I had learned the secret of the pendant and its power.

But my mind was made up. I want to be a normal twelve-year-old girl, I told myself. I don't want to be a freak, running around in a costume every night. I don't want to fight and kill and chase criminals. *I want a normal life!*

I turned and started to walk toward Jada's house. A car rumbled past. I hid behind a tall hedge. I didn't want anyone to see me in the costume.

About a block from the house, I came to a tree that was tilting over the sidewalk. It probably fell during a storm.

I wished for strength again. Leaned my shoulder into the tree trunk—and pushed it back up straight.

As I brushed off my costume, I heard laughter. From high above. I turned and saw Jada in her red costume come swooping down from the sky.

"Shadow Girl—how's it going?" she asked as she landed gently in front of me.

"You didn't tell me the secret," I cried. "You didn't help me at all. I—I could have been killed!"

She laughed. Behind the red mask, her eyes flashed. "You seem to have figured things out," she said.

I heard voices. And saw two narrow beams of light. At the corner, I could see two girls pedaling toward us on bikes.

"Listen, Jada, I want to go home," I said.

"Don't call me Jada. My name is Red Raven."

"I don't care," I insisted. "I don't want to do this. I think superheroes belong in comic books. I don't want to live—"

I stopped when I saw a car roar around the corner. Its headlights swept over the two girls and their bikes.

The shrill squeal of brakes rose over the girls' startled screams. The car skidded hard.

Jada gave me a shove—and I took off.

I leaped across the street. Dove in front of the car. Lowered my shoulder. And took a solid blow as the bumper smashed into my side.

I held my place. I didn't fall back.

The car bounced. Once. Twice. And stopped.

I spun around to see the girls skid onto the grass. One of them fell off her bike. The other one squealed her bike to a stop.

They were okay. I had saved their lives.

A man poked his head out of the car from behind the wheel. "Who are you?" he cried. "How did you *do* that?"

"I'm Shadow Girl!" I declared.

I spun around. Raised my arms high. And took off into the air. Glancing back, I could see the driver's startled face as I sped through the sky.

I came to a gentle landing in Jada's backyard. My shoulder ached from smashing against the bumper. I started to feel sick again.

I dropped to my knees. I pulled up the mask. I couldn't breathe. My stomach churned.

I felt a hand on my shoulder and gazed up at Jada. "You just saved two lives!" she exclaimed. "How did that feel?"

"Terrible," I groaned. "I . . . I hate it, Jada. It makes me sick."

"Too bad," she replied sharply.

I climbed dizzily to my feet.

"Too bad," she repeated. She gave me a hard shove that sent me staggering back.

"Hey—!" I cried out angrily. "What's the big idea?"

"Too bad if you don't want to be Shadow Girl," Jada shouted. "It's what I wanted my whole life—and you want to throw it away."

She shoved me again. I bumped hard into a mail-box post.

"I won't let you!" Jada cried. "I won't let you quit. I'm your enemy. I'm your *arch*-enemy! Why do you think I've been preparing you to be Shadow Girl? So I can defeat you! So I can *destroy* you! Face your fate, Selena! Face it!"

"No—!" I screamed. "No way!"

I dodged to the side as she reached to shove me again.

Our capes tangled together. I tugged mine free and pushed her away.

Behind the mask, her blue eyes went wide. She

opened her mouth in a scream—and threw herself on top of me.

She tackled me to the pavement. I rolled out from under her and swung my body on top of hers. I dove forward, trying to pin her arms to the ground.

Groaning, squirming, kicking, she tried to battle free.

With a shriek, I grabbed her blond hair and tugged hard.

She rolled to the side—and I went tumbling into the street.

And then we were standing up, wrestling, tearing at each other, crying, and groaning in pain.

I let out a horrified shriek when I looked down—and saw the houses and trees far beneath us.

She had pulled me high in the air. And now we fought high above the ground. Kicking at each other. Wrestling. Crying out our anger.

We're both going to fall, I realized. We're both going to die!

"I don't want this! I don't want this!" I shrieked.

"It's your fate!" Jada screamed back.

"Noooo!" I wailed.

And then I realized what I had to do.

Wrestling with my cousin high in the night sky, the winds swirling, battering us as we struggled—I knew what I had to do to end this. To free myself.

"Okay—I'll face my fate!" I screamed. "And now it's time for you to face yours!"

Jada's eyes bulged in surprise.

"I'm going to do as the book said!" I told her. "I'm going to kill you now!"

I reached out—and ripped the red pendant off Jada's throat.

Jada desperately tried to grab it back. "No! Give it back! I need it! I can't *live* without it!"

With a cry, I heaved the pendant to the ground.

I heard it shatter on the pavement beneath us. And I knew that I had killed her.

My scream rang through the night sky. "Die, Red Raven! Die!"

Conclusion

Friday night. A calm, cool night. The trees are still. A bright half-moon sends silvery light over the houses and lawns of Elmwood.

Shadow Girl slid down the tree at the side of the house. Keeping in the blue-black shade of the house, she made her way silently to the front.

She stopped near the curb to adjust her mask. Then she pushed her cape back over her shoulders.

A car rumbled past, its radio blaring country music. She dove behind an evergreen shrub to keep from the glare of the headlights.

Then Shadow Girl crossed the street, her boots clicking on the pavement. A crash from inside the Carver house across the street startled her. She stopped for a second. Then took off, running to the side of the house.

Sure enough, a window had been slid open.

No lights had been turned on. She saw the darting yellow beam of a flashlight cutting through the dark.

Footsteps from the front room. The light swept one way, then another.

Silently, Shadow Girl climbed onto the windowsill. Then she lowered herself into the house.

She landed softly and made her way across the dining room.

A cabinet drawer banged in the front room. More footsteps.

She crept into the living room. Her gloved hand found the light switch on the wall.

She clicked on the ceiling light—and saw the masked figure. He wore a blue cape and had a blue ski mask pulled down over his face. He was bent over the TV set, unplugging it.

He froze when he saw her. Then he raised the flashlight and sent the bright beam into her face.

"Who are you? What are you doing here?" he demanded.

"I'm Shadow Girl," she announced. "This is your last robbery, Blue Weasel."

He stood up slowly, his eyes unblinking, locked on her. "My last robbery? What makes you so sure?"

She didn't reply. Instead, she leaped forward. She batted the flashlight from his hand and then lowered her shoulder to tackle him to the floor.

He dodged quickly. Then he grabbed her cape with both hands.

Shadow Girl caught her balance and spun around to face him.

But the masked burglar twisted the cape around her. Wrapped it around her throat.

She lashed out with both hands. But her punches went wild.

He began to tighten the cape. Tightening it around her throat. Choking off her air.

She raised a knee. Tried to kick him. Thrashed her hands at him.

But she could feel herself growing weak as he tightened the cape even more. Tightened it, choking off her air . . .

Choking her . . .

One last chance. She let her knees buckle. Dropped to the floor. And started to spin.

Faster. Faster.

The burglar stumbled back in surprise as the cape jerked out of his hands.

Shadow Girl rose up, spinning, spinning so hard, she created a whirlwind. The wind whipped around them both, sending the cape sailing around the burglar.

He tried to toss it away. But the swirling wind wrapped the cape around him. Held him in place, tightening like the wraps around a mummy.

The cape held him helpless. Until the whirlwind faded. And Shadow Girl stepped forward to pluck the cape away.

She reached out and pulled off the blue mask.

"I'm so sorry," she whispered. "I'm so sorry it's you, Stan."

His face darkened to beet red. His eyes rolled crazily in his head. "How—how did you know?" he cried hoarsely.

"Shadow Girl knows everything," she replied, and dragged him out of the house.

● ● ●

I stood in the bushes at the bottom of the yard and watched Jada lead Stan away. At first, I couldn't believe my eyes.

Stan? Stan was the Blue Weasel?

Did Jada know this all along?

The mask hid Jada's eyes. But I could see the smile on her face. I knew she was enjoying being a superhero.

I was smiling too. I knew I had done the right thing.

Later, I waited in the secret room for Jada to return. It was nearly midnight when I heard her climb the tree. She dropped gracefully in through the window.

"You waited up for me?" she asked, straightening her black cloak.

I nodded. "I had to talk to you. Did you know that Stan was the burglar all along?"

"Yes," she replied with a sigh. "Poor guy. It was too easy. You know. The new DVD player. The new computer. Stan's family is so poor. How could they afford all that?"

We both dropped to the floor to talk, resting our backs against the wall.

"So I told Stan about the Carvers being away all week," Jada continued. "I made up a story about throwing a party there Saturday night. I knew he'd go there to rob it before the party because he knew the house was empty. It was such an easy trap."

I laughed. "Easy for *you* maybe—but not for me. I'm glad I killed you. You make a much better Shadow Girl than I ever would."

My cousin sighed. "Yes, Red Raven is dead. Gone forever. When you gave your pendant and costume to me, I became Shadow Girl for all time—for the rest of my life."

"I'm sorry it took me so long to figure out what to do," I said. "I was so confused."

"You had to discover it for yourself," she replied. "You had to hand over the costume of your own free will. And when you did, I truly became Shadow Girl."

"I'm so happy we both got what we want!" I exclaimed.

And we threw our arms around each other and hugged—hugged for real—for the first time in our lives.

I returned home a few days later, and Mom was very surprised to see me. So surprised, she dropped an entire tray of glasses!

Of course, there was a lot of hugging and crying.

Through my tears, I did my best to explain.

Mom agreed that I had done the right thing. But she had an odd expression on her face. I had the weirdest feeling that she was disappointed somehow.

But that had to be my imagination.

"I'm so glad to return to a normal life!" I cried. And more hugs and tears followed.

After we talked for a while longer, I made my way to the stairs. "I have to call Beth," I said. "I have to tell her the good news that I'm back. That we can be friends again."

I ran up the stairs. I was passing Mom's room on the way to mine, when I spotted something on the bed.

Something weird.

I stepped into Mom's room and hurried over to the bed.

To my surprise, Mom burst into the room behind me. Her face was twisted in horror.

"You weren't supposed to see that!" she cried. "I didn't know you were coming home. I would have put it in its place."

My heart pounding, I picked it up. A red cape. A pair of silky red tights. A sparkly black mask with diamond-shaped eye holes.

"Mom? What *is* it?" I cried.

"My costume," she said in a whisper.

ABOUT THE AUTHOR

R.L. STINE says he has a great job. "My job is to give kids the CREEPS!" With his scary books, R.L. has terrified kids all over the world. He has sold over 300 million books, making him the best-selling children's author in history.

These days, R.L. is dishing out new frights in his series THE NIGHTMARE ROOM. When he isn't working, he likes to read old mysteries, watch *SpongeBob Squarepants* on TV, and take his dog, Nadine, for long walks around New York City, where he lives with his wife, Jane, and son, Matthew.

Take a look at what's ahead in
THE NIGHTMARE ROOM #9
Camp Nowhere

I didn't scream.

I was proud of that. I think maybe that's one reason no one teased me about the wasps later.

The sting only swelled a little bit. It itched a lot. But the cream that Ramos spread over it kept it from really hurting.

"You were lucky," Ramos said later, as we paddled along the river, the current pulling us easily. "All those wasps and only one sting. The others must have decided that you wrecked their nest by accident."

I forced a weak laugh. "I guess."

"You were brave, the way you just froze there and let them climb all over you," Charlotte said. She shuddered. "Just thinking about it gives me the creeps."

The river picked up speed. We took turns paddling. The sun tried to come out a few times. But it couldn't break through the high clouds.

My neck was throbbing and I felt a little dizzy by the time Ramos announced it was time to stop for the day. We pulled the canoes to a wide, grassy area on the shore.

Then we carried the tents and other supplies across the grass to a flat, dry circle surrounded by tall trees. I saw a rabbit watching us from the edge of the woods. Two cawing bluejays swooped through the low branches of the trees.

The air carried a chill. The sky darkened to charcoal gray.

"We need lots of firewood," Ramos instructed. "After we cook our food, we'll want to keep the fire going for warmth. Get going, guys."

He set to work on the tents. The five of us made our way into the woods.

I was walking with David and Marty. But when I bent down to pick up some long twigs, they wandered away. I saw the two girls on the other side of a clump of tall reeds. They were struggling to pick up a fat log from the ground.

"Russell—find any wasps' nests?" Marty called.

"Not yet!" I shouted back.

"We're staying as far away from you as we can," David said.

Erin said something, but I couldn't hear her. I was staring at something caught in the brambles of a low bush.

At first I thought it was a small, white bird. But bending down, I saw that it was an arrow. A stone arrow with a long, white feather attached. "Weird," I muttered.

I picked it up to study it. Was it an Indian arrow?

"Hey—check this out!" Charlotte called. Carrying the arrow, I hurried over to her. She held up a small, brown object. "I found it resting against that tree."

"A doll?" I asked.

She nodded. "It's made of some kind of leather. And it's wearing a long dress, all fringed."

"It's an Indian papoose," Erin said, taking it from Charlotte.

I showed them the feathered arrow. "Remember? Indians lived in these woods for hundreds of years," I said.

"But these things are brand new," Erin replied.

"How could that be?" Charlotte asked, studying the arrow, running her finger over the fresh, white feather. "Ramos told us the Indians were driven out a hundred years ago. So how did these things get here?"

"It's a mystery," Erin said. She handed the little, leather doll back to Charlotte. "A real mystery."

I heard Indian drums again that night.

We all gobbled up dinner—hot dogs on the fire and sandwiches left over from lunch. We were starving.

We showed Ramos the doll and the feathered arrow. But he couldn't explain them. He was as puzzled as we were.

After dinner, Ramos asked if we wanted to sit

around and tell jokes. But we were all yawning. Aching and exhausted from the long day of canoe paddling.

The tents formed a tight circle around the fire. The shadows of the flames danced on the vinyl tent walls.

We divided up and climbed wearily into the tents. Marty and I shared a tent. I left the tent flap open so that we could watch the fire and feel its heat.

We pulled off our muddy boots. Then we climbed into our sleeping bags in our clothes.

"How is your wasp sting?" Marty asked, yawning.

"Not too bad," I whispered. "It itches a little, but it's okay."

I turned and saw that he was sound asleep.

I settled into the sleeping bag and stared out at the red-orange flames licking up at the darkness.

A minute or so later, the drumbeats began.

Low and distant. A slow, steady *thrum . . . thrum . . . thrum*.

Indian drums, I thought.

I pictured the leather doll, the feathered arrow.

I picked up my head and gazed out through the tent flap. The fire had died down. The flames were small now, sparks above the purple embers.

Thrum . . . thrum . . . thrum . . .

Soft drumbeats from the woods. From all around.

All around the circle of the clearing, I thought.

Thrum . . . thrum . . .

Soft but close . . . so close.

I fell asleep to the slow, steady rhythm of the drumbeats. I slept a deep, dreamless sleep.

I jerked awake the next morning—sat straight up—stared out at the gray morning light.

What woke me up?

A scream?

Yes. A hideous, deafening scream of pain.

Ramos!

I reached over and frantically shook Marty awake.

"Wake up!" I cried. "It's Ramos! Do you hear that scream? It's Ramos!"

Ramos's screams echoed off the trees.

I pulled on my boots and scrambled out of the tent.

Charlotte and Erin were awake, standing tensely in front of the dead campfire. Charlotte's red hair stood out in all directions. Erin was struggling to tug down the sleeves of her sweatshirt.

They turned to me, their eyes wide with fright. Marty hopped out of the tent, pulling on his left boot.

David came climbing out of the tent he shared with Ramos. "What's happening?" he asked, his voice still hoarse from sleep. "Is that Ramos screaming?"

Before anyone could answer, Ramos roared across the clearing, holding his right arm tightly against his side. His face was red. His dark eyes were half shut from pain.

"Oh, man. Oh, man," he moaned.

"Ramos—what happened?" Charlotte cried. We all ran across the grass toward him.

"My arm," he moaned. "I—I think I tore something."

He dropped into a sitting position in front of the dead fire. "Oh, man—it hurts." He gripped the arm tightly, holding it stiffly against him.

We huddled around him. "What happened? What did you do to it?" I asked.

He groaned in pain. "I went out early to chop more firewood for this morning," he said. He looked around. "Where's the ax? Oh, man. I left it in the woods."

"I'll go get it," I said.

He motioned for me to stay where I was. "I was chopping a log in two—and I heard something snap. In my arm. The pain is *unbelievable*!"

He motioned to David. "Bring me some water. It's in the pack over there. I . . . I'm so dry."

"Do you think you broke your arm?" Marty asked him.

David handed the water bottle to Ramos. Ramos tilted it to his mouth and took a long drink. "No. I didn't break the bone," he said, wincing in pain. "I think I tore the tendon."

He drank down the rest of the water and crushed the plastic bottle in his good hand. "I can't believe this," he muttered. "I won't be able to paddle at all."

My heart jumped. "Do you mean we have to go back to camp?" I asked.

Ramos shook his head. He glanced at the river. "No. We're too close. The falls are less than half an hour away. You . . . you'll just have to go over them without me."

I gasped. I could feel my stomach tighten. "Go without you?" I whispered.

Holding his arm, Ramos struggled to his feet. "I'm really sorry I won't be able to help. But you guys can do it without me. I know you can."

"But—if we get in trouble . . ." Erin started. "If we need help . . ."

"You'll help each other," Ramos told her. He groaned in pain. "Listen, guys—leave everything here. We'll pick it up on the way back. Just have some breakfast. Get into your life jackets. Take the two canoes. And go."

"But where will you be?" I asked.

"I'm going to start walking now," he answered. "I'll wait for you down below the falls. I'll be watching the whole thing from the shore."

"But, Ramos—" Erin started.

"No more questions," he groaned. "Good luck, everyone. Make me proud."

Holding his arm limply at his side, Ramos turned and started away, walking quickly. We watched him make his way out of the clearing.

When he reached the shore, he gazed at the

canoes for a moment. Then he turned and started to follow the river.

He didn't look back.

The five of us didn't say anything for a while.

Marty kicked the crushed water bottle into the fire. The bottle sent up a cloud of ashes.

"Guess we might as well get going," Charlotte said.

"Yeah," I said softly. "Let's get it over with." A shiver ran down my back. "We can do it . . . right?"

Our paddles splashed the water. The canoe felt empty without Ramos.

I sat in the back. Charlotte took the middle. I raised the paddles, then pushed. . . . Raised the paddles, then pushed. Copying Charlotte's rhythm.

Trying not to think about where we were headed.

My life jacket seemed to weigh a hundred pounds. Large drops of sweat started to roll down my forehead, stinging my eyes.

Through the morning gray, I saw a tall deer, watching us from the shore. The sun, trying to poke through the clouds, cast a white glare over the flowing water.

The canoe rocked as water splashed up in front of us. The current is definitely speeding up, I realized.

The river grew wider. The tangled trees along the banks suddenly seemed a lot farther away.

I leaned forward and paddled harder. Our two

canoes slid through the water side by side.

"Whoa!" I cried out as we tossed over an onrushing wave. The canoe slapped the water hard as it came back down.

Swirls of water made circles of white foamy waves. The canoe bumped again, harder this time.

"We're getting close," Marty said. "The river is starting to get rough."

A wave of fear swept over me. We need Ramos for this, I thought. It isn't safe to be doing this on our own.

I wondered if the others were thinking the same thing.

I was so surprised when Erin spoke up. "Maybe we should turn back," she said. "I don't feel right without Ramos. I mean, what if one of us falls into the river? What if our canoes crack up on the rocks?"

"Erin, go climb in Russell's canoe!" David joked. "The two of you could hold each other's hands."

"Not funny," Erin snapped.

Our canoes tossed up, then slapped back down.

"Russell, are you getting seasick?" David asked.

"No way! This is fun!" I lied. "I hope it gets rougher than this. This is kind of babyish."

I'm going to be the bravest one here, I vowed to myself. Even if it *kills* me!

Foamy, white water tossed up in front of us, then splashed down into the canoe. The canoe rocked from side to side as water slapped the sides.

I bounced into the air and nearly dropped one of my paddles. Charlotte's hair flew wildly behind her head. Our faces were wet from the cold spray.

"Guys, I'm serious!" Erin shouted. "This is too scary! And we haven't even come to the falls!"

I was so glad she was saying this, and not me. But would anyone listen?

"Erin, just keep paddling," Marty said. "You'll be okay. Really."

"We won't be okay!" Erin cried, her voice shrill and trembling. "We're going over steep falls, and we're going to crash into rocks below!"

Charlotte suddenly spoke up. "We have to do this!" she shouted, bouncing up as a wave tossed the canoe. "We can't be the first senior campers in history not to go over Forbidden Falls!"

"But the others all had a counselor with them!" Erin protested.

"So we'll be the first *without* a counselor!" I shouted. "We'll be famous!"

Everyone turned to look at me. "Russell—you're the man!" Marty yelled. "You're the man!"

We all had to shout over the roar of the water. White-foamed waves tossed against the canoes on all sides. The canoes bounced beneath us.

Our canoe went into a wild spin. Charlotte and I stabbed the paddles harder and held firm. "Whooooaaa!" We both laughed as the canoe finally straightened itself.

Paddling hard, I turned to the other canoe. Marty sat in front. He was drenched with water. His hair was matted to his head. Water rose up into the canoe. Splashed against the front of his life jacket.

Erin, in the middle, leaned forward. She seemed to be ducking behind Marty, letting him shield her. Her face was very pale in the gray light. Even from my boat, I could see the fear tightening her face.

David stared straight ahead. His eyes were narrowed. His face was set. His body was tensed, alert, ready for anything. As the canoe bounced and rocked, his expression didn't change.

Our canoe bumped down hard, then bumped again, as if going down steep stairs. "We—we're almost there!" I shouted to Charlotte.

She shouted a reply, but I couldn't hear her over the roar of the rushing water. The canoe shot forward, rocking harder. The current pulled us faster . . . faster.

"Look out!" I shouted as the swirling waves tossed the canoe at the shore. "Too close!"

Tall, gray rocks jutted up along both sides of the riverbank.

We struggled to paddle back to the middle. The river curved sharply here, and the current kept pushing us to the shore.

The falls are right around this curve, I remembered.

Cold water splashed over me. I gasped and sucked in a shuddering breath.

So close . . .

We're seconds away, I knew. Seconds away from Forbidden Falls.

The river curved sharply. The rushing current carried us forward, faster . . . faster . . .

Charlotte and I stopped paddling. I gripped the sides tightly, holding on for dear life.

"Here we go. *Here we go!*"

I tried to remember Ramos' instructions. But they had flown out of my head.

I couldn't remember. I couldn't think.

I couldn't move.

The rushing water roared in my ears. Waves rose up all around us, as if reaching for us. The canoe tilted to one side, heaving me hard. I felt myself start to tumble out.

Then the canoe tilted to the other side. I fell back into place.

Charlotte's hair flew in the wind, flapping behind her like a red pennant.

I turned to see the others. But their canoe had fallen behind us.

Charlotte and I were going down first!

The river curved . . . curved again . . .

And as the falls came into view, I couldn't help it.

I opened my mouth in a deafening, shrill scream.